FINDING HOME

DIANA DERICCI

Purple Sword Publications
Tucson, AZ

FINDING HOME
Copyright © 2015 DIANA DERICCI
ISBN 978-1-61292-145-7
ISBN 10: 1612921450
Cover Art Designed by Anastasia Rabiyah
Edited by Traci Markou

Published by Purple Sword Publications, LLC
Tucson, Arizona, USA
www.PurpleSword.com

The Jasper Series
Reading List:

Tougher to Love
Second Chance Summer
Finding Home
Finding Family

Dedication:

I want to sincerely thank Parker W. for letting me not only hijack his names for this story, but for doing it with a humored graciousness.

Sometimes that imaginary line in the sand is the only thing stopping you from loving.

Chapter One

Parker hefted his backpack onto a shoulder, his other arm held out with his thumb up. The passing vehicle didn't even slow down. The hot cyclone of dry air it left in its wake made him grimace. He paused to let it rush beyond him as the sultry August heat beat down on him. He was used to walking. Except every now and then, a cool car would be welcome.

He adjusted the large cowboy hat on his head and started moving again. Forward. He never wanted to go in reverse again. Why be somewhere after you've already been there? He wanted to go where he'd never been, and that was in front of him. Never behind.

Parker walked through the noonday heat into the afternoon. He held out his thumb, though no one ever stopped. They hardly did anymore. Not that he could blame them. People died making goodwill efforts. He couldn't imagine doing anything like that. He hated to fight. Hated to hurt others. If those facts made him a pussy, then so be it. Lord knew his father had called him that and worse over the years.

He stopped under a shade tree a few yards from the road, resting, aware he was rambling in his thoughts. Sunstroke, dehydration, and no food. Not a good combination for a lone man traversing the country's highways.

Sinking to the ground, he fanned his face with his hat. His boots were dusty. He was filthy. He'd forgotten what a hot shower felt like. Idly, he played with a loose side tooth with the tip of his tongue. Sooner or later, he'd have to do something about it. One too many hits from his dad. It was getting worse, which wasn't a good sign.

A beat up truck slowed at the roadside. He didn't blink, waiting. There was a grinding, metallic creak as a window rolled down to expose the driver. A gnarled older man that had to be eighty if he was a day leaned on the wheel.

"You need a ride, boy? You's lookin' mighty peak-ed."

Parker nodded.

"How far you goin'?"

"As far as you can take me." He'd never had a destination.

"Climb in the back." He hooked a thumb over a shoulder. Parker stood at the offer. "I can get you to Jasper. It's apiece up the road yet."

It wasn't AC, but it wasn't walking. Parker nodded grimly. "Appreciated."

He tossed his hat and backpack over the truck sidewall then hefted himself in to sit behind the cab. He rested an arm over an upright, bent knee.

The driver spoke through the rear cab window before getting a good speed up. "Name's Grint. I'd let you up here, but I'm driving to see my grandbaby. Daughter will have a might fit if the truck is filthy."

The old man's grumbling made him smile. "I don't mind. Thanks for the ride."

"You's welcome. Hang on back there. I'll let you know when we hit town."

Parker closed his eyes. It wasn't so bad. The chance to rest helped. He didn't know how long they drove. He didn't have a watch or a phone. In the grand scheme of his world, neither mattered.

He jerked and blinked his eyes when the driver's door slammed shut. "Wake up. This is as far as I can take you."

Parker swiveled on his neck taking in the town in a first glance. "Jasper, huh?"

"It ain't N'Awlins," the old man scoffed, then cackled a dry laugh like he'd made a knee slapper of a joke.

Parker slung his pack over a shoulder and crammed his hat on his head, gliding over the edge to land on his feet. "Thanks, Grint." He went to shake, but faltered.

The man held out a twenty dollar bill. "Here, son. You need this more than I do today."

"I can't take your money." He attempted to back away, smacking into the truck behind him.

"When you have it, give it t'a person who needs it more 'an you." Grint managed to stuff it in his front pocket, ignoring his refusals. "Two doors from the bakery is grub. Get a meal 'afore you take off outta town 'gain."

With that, Grint turned and walked down the sidewalk to one of the other storefronts, leaving him standing there on the sidewalk confused. The kindness of strangers never ceased to amaze him. He pushed fingers into his pocket, feeling the stiff crispness of the bill.

It was real. He bowed his head and sent a silent thank you to Grint for being bothered enough to stop today.

He looked the way Grint had told him to go, making out the red and white striped banner that had to be the bakery. Self-conscious of his disheveled state, he hurried as quickly as he could past doors, spotting the entry for the restaurant. White script on the door proclaimed it to be Lucy's. He hoped they didn't turn him away because he was a walking wreck.

Just as he reached the door, ready to put his best foot forward and hopefully get to eat, he spotted the large cop at the register. Beige on brown uniform, the thick, black holster belt that sat at his hips, and the two pairs of black steel cuffs clipped on the back. He did an about face that made him dizzy and he stumbled a step.

Parker tried to take another step, reaching for something to firm his balance against. He found air. Sweat broke out on his forehead. Noise vacuumed to his own harsh panting and nothing else. He swayed as his knees turned to water.

"Hey, easy there!" Strong hands captured him at the waist. "Here, sit down and put your head between your knees."

He sank numbly to the curb and did as told. He'd learned a long time ago, acquiescing early on meant less pain later. "I didn't do anything," he croaked, shivering. He hated being roughed by the law. *Hated* it.

"Just breathe," said the soothing, deep voice.

"Is he okay?"

"Don't know yet." That was the man behind him. Calm, in charge.

"Officer Drew? Wha'cha doin' t'a that young'un?"

Parker recognized that voice. Grint.

"Nothing."

Parker caught the motion as a beige leg and more than likely the body it was attached to moved into his vision to talk to Grint, yet the hand on his shoulder remained.

So it wasn't the cop holding him down.

"Think you can sit up now?" Still calm. Unaggressive. Parker knew better than to trust it. He was too outnumbered.

Parker nodded silently. He grasped his hat and held it in his hands, trying to look around. The cop, the man behind him, Grint, and a lady he could only guess was his daughter holding a young toddler.

"Sorry," Parker mumbled.

"You gonna let that boy go eat, Ian? He ain't hurtin' nuthin'."

"Making sure he's okay," he said loud enough to be heard. "Are you okay?" he gently asked Parker.

Parker nodded. The man stood and offered a hand. Looking at how dirty his were, Parker studied the man's, Ian's, and noticed he had a mechanic's hands. Some professions you could tell by a man's hands. He had no idea whose could be worse at that moment. He clasped the hand above him and found his feet.

"I have to get back on the clock." The cop came and stood at Ian's shoulder.

Ian turned and gazed over a shoulder into the man's eyes. A hand lifted and touched his chin. Parker spotted the ring on his finger when he did. "See you at home."

"Love you," the cop whispered. Ian touched the cop's lip with a fleeting fingertip, and then he was gone.

Parker started trembling again. He also noticed Grint and his daughter were getting into the truck to leave. Parker wanted to leave with them. He didn't even care where. He didn't want to be right there, right this second.

"You sure you're okay?"

"Food," Parker stammered, knowing he was staring wild-eyed at the glass doors in front of him. Escape.

Ian nodded. "Probably been a while, huh?"

Parker tipped to stare at him. He was a couple of inches too short to get a good eye view meeting. "I can pay." *Now.* "I'm not a thief."

"I want to help you, but you need to be honest with me. Keep in mind, my husband is a Sheriff."

It felt as though Parker swallowed through glass. *Husband?* Parker was sure he was about to faint, and it wasn't all heat induced. He tipped his head once, trying to stay on his feet.

"Are you over eighteen?"

"Yes," he whispered, keeping his gaze down. He clutched at his backpack, his hat crumpled in his other fist.

"Are you wanted?"

"No."

Ian's hands had risen to his hips after a nerve-stretching pause. "I don't need lengthy explanations unless you want to give them. Let's get you some hot food."

"Why?"

"Why?" Ian halted his turn, frowning for reasons Parker couldn't begin to know, but feared he could guess.

"Why are you doing this? Anything?"

"Because you almost passed out at my feet." Then he turned and opened the glass door wide, waiting for him.

Parker trudged in behind him.

"Lucy, can we get a hot plate to go?" he spoke to the lady at the register.

When Parker reached in his pocket for the bill Grint had given him, Ian stayed his hand with a touch to his wrist.

"Put it on Caleb's coffee bill, would you?"

"You betcha." She wrote a note by the register and then dashed to the back.

Parker really wanted to sit down. Instead he shifted from one foot then to the other, trying to stay upright. That dizzy spell had drained him. It had been a while since he'd had one. Since he hadn't eaten recently, it really sucker punched him.

The scents reaching him were divine: fresh bread, hot meats, gravy, potatoes, but he knew better than to try to move past the guy at his shoulder. He should have known they wouldn't want him inside. Wasn't the first time he'd been called a health hazard in the three plus years he'd been walking.

"Hang on, just a little longer." Ian was watching him again. His voice was calm, that soothing note in it again. It made no difference to Parker whether he stayed there or not. He could sit under a bridge somewhere and eat as easily as at a table. Ian was being kind to get him a hot dinner, at least. It meant he could stretch the twenty in his pocket a little further.

It wasn't like he hadn't earned his meals from time to time. Washing dishes, mopping, whatever. He tried not to think too often of the times he'd had to sell himself for a couple of bucks to get that hot meal. He was even gladder that he'd never been attacked or mugged. If people were hurt giving help, many more of them died needing it.

He didn't know how long they stood by the front of the restaurant when she came bustling up from the kitchen. "Here you go, sugar. There's an extra corn bread and a slice of apple pie."

"Thanks, Lucy." Ian reached for the hefty bag.

"Poor baby. He's dead on his feet."

Parker heard her, but pretended he didn't. "Thank you, ma'am," he said, meaning it while he eyed the bag in Ian's grip.

"Let's go." Ian held the door again.

Only he didn't stop walking once they were outside. Walking away with Parker's food.

"Wait!" He hurried to catch up. "I can carry it." His stomach grumbled like a sleepy volcano as scents rose from the paper bag. The same ones from the restaurant. His mouth salivated like a faucet. He was shocked. He didn't think he had any moisture in him to spare.

Ian didn't answer, simply started moving again.

Dutifully, Parker trailed the man because he knew that was what Ian wanted and what he had to do if he wanted what was in that bag.

Chapter Two

Ian knew he was being cruel, but sometimes you have to be cruel to be kind, as the old song went. He reached his pickup and unlocked the passenger door. "Inside."

"What? Why?" The young man lurched to a stop, his tired eyes going wild-colt wide.

"One, I'm not going to let you sleep on the ground somewhere. Two, I have your dinner." Then he sauntered around to the driver's side and unlocked that door to climb in.

"I'll make it dirty," he said so quietly, Ian wasn't even sure he'd spoken.

"Son, look at this truck. Look at me. Do you think dirty is a concern?" Ian had owned this truck for almost twenty years. It showed in the grimy seats, the lingering smell of motor oil, and the dark smudges on everything, but it ran and the AC kicked ass. That was all he cared about.

He shut his door and cranked the motor. The bag was placed on the center board, out of the way. Gingerly, the young man joined him, sloughing off his pack to rest on the floorboards, his hat on top of that.

"I know you aren't going to trust me," Ian said once they were moving. "I don't blame you, either. You can clean up, eat, and if you have to run as soon as you're done, then I can't stop you." He adjusted his visor for the sun. A hot August evening that he hoped would start cooling soon.

"Thank you."

He had a very rich Texas twang, but was soft spoken. Ian sighed. "I'm not going to hurt you."

Ian mulled over what he was doing, and wished the damned kid wasn't tugging at his heartstrings so hard. He had enough family with Caleb's nephews and his own niece. Since marrying Caleb, they'd become the cool uncles. Jessie's boys loved coming to stay with them, why he honestly didn't know, other than they simply could get away from home. And that wasn't counting their goddaughter, whom they got to babysit on occasion. It was as close to fatherhood of the miniature species Ian wanted to get.

He simply couldn't leave him. Ian wasn't made that way.

"You're Ian?" he asked.

"Yes. My husband is Caleb."

He saw the youngster swallow hard when he used the word again. "I know. It's not normal," Ian retorted. He rolled tight fists around the cracked plastic steering wheel. He honestly didn't care what anyone thought any longer. Not after six years with the man. He was who he was. No one else had to live Ian's life.

"No!" The boy whipped around and clutched his hands on his lap. "I—It surprised me."

"Well, if you have a problem eating in a gay man's house, I'll let you out now." He lifted his foot off the gas pedal.

"No! I swear."

"Good." Because they were almost home.

He pulled into the drive behind Caleb's car. It was so rarely used anymore, but he refused to sell it.

"Grab your things." He grasped the bag of food before the kid could. He knew the best way to keep the kid following, like a hungry puppy that was skittish of being handled. Ian caught the way his hand trembled as he scooped up the handle of his pack. He knew a lot of that had to do with the need for the food Ian carried. Exhaustion. Fear. He couldn't imagine what the boy had probably lived through. He didn't think he wanted to.

"Set your things there." He pointed to a spot by the wall once they were inside. Within reach, and easily seen. He hoped that made him at least a little comfortable.

Ian placed the food bag on the table. "The bathroom is around the hall on the right. Just wash up to eat for now."

The boy shakily slid from the kitchen, his eyes barely leaving the bag. While he was gone, Ian got everything on the table for him, including a large bottle of water and tea to drink. He didn't think he'd be long, and he wasn't.

"Go ahead and sit."

He did. A single look to see if the container was going to suddenly be yanked, and it wasn't, was all he needed to dive into the food.

"Do you have a name?" Ian asked, remembering to keep his voice even and smooth. He may have been sitting, but he was still in flight mode.

"Parker," he replied, stuffing his mouth full of mashed potatoes.

Ian leaned against the sink counter, watching him inhale the prepared dinner. He'd said he was over eighteen, but Ian didn't think he was much over it. By the condition he was in, the wear on his clothes, the drawn thinness of his face, he guessed he'd been out on the road for a while.

The mere thought of something like this happening to Terra, or Becky, or any of the boys... It's why when Maria had died, he had no doubts about taking in Terra. She was his family. And he would have hated himself if this had been her outcome.

He didn't know Parker's story, why he was homeless. He guessed it wasn't a happy, feel-good kind of story, and he doubted in all reality that his time out in the world had been a picnic.

"Ow!"

Parker dropped the fork to the table and cupped his face. He was breathing heavily, obviously in pain.

"What happened?" He didn't think he'd ever found a bone in Lucy's roast, but what did he know about cooking?

"I have a bad tooth," he mumbled. "Dad knocked it loose and it never healed."

Ian managed to control the flashed urge to find the asshole that would hit his own kid. Instead, he leaned close, pushing the water toward him. "Drink some of this. It will hurt, but it will dull the pain afterward."

Parker carefully did, wincing at the icy coldness. "Any better?"

"Little." He placed the bottle on the table and found his fork. He started eating again. A little slower, and more cautiously of how and where.

"How long has it been like that?"

"A while now. I don't know when he knocked it loose, exactly. It happened more than once."

Ian's cell phone rang, and Parker paused in his eating. It was probably good to have an interruption.

He couldn't believe how angry hearing how Parker's father had abused the boy made him.

"It's okay." He waved to Parker to keep eating after a quick peek at the screen. "Hi, Terra."

"Hi, Uncle Ian." She giggled profusely.

"What happened?" He rolled his eyes, waiting for the deluge. But he heard, "He proposed!" instead followed by a not too soft, very feminine shriek of excitement.

Ian shook his head, smiling goofily. Everyone in the family saw this coming. He was glad a summer romance that had started so long ago had stayed strong through all the years of school and distance.

"I'm happy, honey. Thrilled."

"Is Uncle Caleb home?"

"Not yet."

"Can you tell him? I'm going to be a little tied up..."

Terra's voice drifted away as a playful growl reached Ian's ear. "Hi, Uncle Ian."

He laughed. "Hi, Aaron. Be good to my girl."

"Always," he replied. "I'll have her call in a few days for a get-together. Think Uncle Caleb and you can make it?"

"Should be able to. Give me warning. Oh! Have you told Brice and Jake?" He was pretty sure Jessie was a foregone conclusion. Aaron's dad would tan his hide for *not* being in the grapevine on this one.

"They're next," she said, getting back into the conversation. "Love you!"

"Love you, too. Bye."

He hung up the phone, slipping it into his pocket. That was news to tell Caleb face to face.

"Your daughter?" Parker asked tentatively.

"Niece. Her boyfriend proposed."

"That's nice." He went back to eating.

Ian noticed he'd reached the bottom of the container compartments and was working on the corn bread for the juices. If he hadn't already eaten, he'd want some of that for himself. Since Lucy had opened her restaurant, her roast had become a city treasure.

"How is your tooth?"

"Achy."

Ian went to the bathroom and found the pain relievers. "Do you have any allergies?" he asked, coming back into the room.

"Not that I know of."

"These will help." He put the bottle by his food container.

Parker lifted the pill bottle and rolled it in his palm. Silence stretched. "Why are you doing this?"

"Because you need it." Ian drew out a chair and sat at the top of the table. "Since I've been with Caleb, I've seen a lot of things I wish I could fix. He volunteers at the homeless shelter and helps the PFLAG and GSA kids at the high school. I never really paid much attention to it, because I wasn't even out. Then I met Caleb."

Parker was still eating, though slowly, as he paid attention.

"I knew some of the pain, but my experiences were twenty, thirty years old. Times have changed. I help now when I can, and so does Caleb's brother and his husband."

Parker whipped up and blinked. "Two gay brothers?"

"Well," Ian chuckled, "Jake is bi, but he's over the moon for Brice. So it doesn't matter to me *why*.

You need something right now. I'm willing to help, if I can."

"And how do I pay you?" He swept an anxious glance toward the front of the house. "I'm guessing you won't be asking for sexual favors."

Ian had heard it before but it still took him aback. "No," he said firmly. "And if any person does, you tell me or Caleb. It doesn't matter that you're over eighteen. You are not to make that bargain." He flushed, leaning away when he realized how strong he was coming across. "Sorry. I'm used to laying ground rules with Terra."

"Honestly, that's one I don't think I mind." Parker's flash of distaste proved he wasn't unknowledgeable in how that kind of bargain worked.

"So, let's do this. I can take you to the homeless shelter. They'll set you up for the night and see you have a bed." He was surprised when Parker's face was accepting, his fork lowering. Like it was what he'd expected. "Or, you make an honest effort to get back on your feet and see how things look in a few weeks. I could use a spare hand at the shop for cleaning up if you think you're capable enough." He clasped his hands on the table, letting the words sink in. Caleb was probably going to skin him alive for making such a gut-instinct decision, especially without talking to him about it first.

"That is unless you like the vagabond lifestyle. I hear there's an entire network city to city for people to connect."

"There is?" he said, breathlessly stunned.

"That's what I've heard. Personally, I don't know. I've been here my whole life."

Parker gaped at him. "You never wanted to leave?"

"I did to go to school, but no, not really. My family was here until they passed, and then I had my business, then Terra."

"I couldn't stay in Galveston." His gaze dropped like a rock to the table.

Ian didn't poke at that. He'd tell when he was ready. He was positive it had a lot do with his father's fist. "It's up to you, Parker. If you want to keep going, I won't stop you. If you want a chance to regroup, you can."

"Where will I sleep?"

"On the porch," Ian told him off the cuff.

Parker's eyes bulged so huge, Ian roared with laughter. He gulped air, calming the sound before trying to talk again.

"I'm kidding! Sorry. That was so wrong. You'll have Terra's old room. There will be some rules to living here. You might want to hear them before you agree," he finished with a tad more seriousness in his tone.

"Okay." He scowled, not amused at Ian's humor.

"No drugs, and we don't drink hard liquor. Caleb is the law, so we don't piss off the law."

"I understand."

"No late nights. I'm sorry, but you'll have to live with two old men who like to go to bed early."

Parker snickered. "Can't be that old. Now Grint, he *is* old."

"Grint is older than dirt," Ian agreed, laughing with him. "If you decide to stay, you'll start paying rent for the room and I'll pay you a wage for working."

"You're kidding?"

"You need experience and a work history."

Parker rubbed lightly over his jaw then popped open the pill bottle to take two with a swallow of tea. "True," he finally agreed. "I had a job before I left home, but that was a long time ago."

"If you decide you want to move on, then I'll pay you for what you've done and we'll call it even."

"Just like that?"

Ian rolled a shoulder. "Not much different from what I would do for a work program for the shelter, only they wouldn't be living here."

"How is your—" there was only the slightest stumble "—husband going to take me being here?"

"Honestly, I don't know. I don't make impulsive decisions like this."

"Then maybe I should go." Parker pushed the scant remains of his dinner away. He looked utterly crestfallen, like a prize had been yanked out of reach.

"Maybe you should give him a chance to understand," Ian offered. "He doesn't bite."

Ian was taking a big chance that the concern he'd seen in Caleb's eyes before he'd left for work after dinner had meant something. Caleb had a big heart, too. Except Ian didn't know if it was this kind of big.

Chapter Three

Caleb finished the paperwork on the last ticket of the evening sitting in his car. He touched the mike on his shoulder. "Oh-four to Dispatch."

"Go ahead, Sheriff Drew."

"I'm done for the night."

"Ten-four. See you tomorrow."

Caleb tossed his clipboard to the passenger seat and made a U-turn on Hoss Road. *Crazy kids.* He sighed and grumbled at the same time, a learned talent of the profession, it seemed. Small towns bred boredom. He got that. Racing cars was not a good way to beat it.

He wasn't surprised when he pulled up in front of the house to see the lights on. Ian usually waited for him if he didn't have to be up early the next morning. After unlatching his computer and all his equipment, he stuffed it in the carryall and then locked the cruiser door when he was out. He was tired, but at least second shift wasn't the overnight any longer.

He opened the front door and walked in. "Babe," he called.

Ian sauntered from the rear of the house. *Damn.* Even after six years, the man could turn Caleb's head in those jeans.

"Hi." Ian greeted him with a kiss that made coming home so fucking wonderful. When Ian moved away, he gathered up Caleb's things out of his hands.

"Go change. There's something I need to talk to you about."

"Sure." Caleb got one more kiss before walking toward the bedroom. The out of place sound didn't register until he was in the hallway.

Terra's shower was running. And Terra was in Texas with Aaron.

Caleb frowned, too tired for much, and not sure he was going to like any explanation.

He changed out of his uniform, taking the precaution to hang his belt and weapon in the closet—something he hadn't done in years. It wasn't locked up, but it wasn't in sight, either. Dressed in shorts and a loose T-shirt, he found his guy in the kitchen.

Ian was wiping down the kitchen sink, a quirk Caleb had learned meant the man had something heavy on his mind. Caleb looped his arms around Ian's still trim waist. He'd put on a couple extra pounds over the years but he wasn't round or soft and had *finally* discovered a few gray hairs. Caleb had him hands down in that department. Caleb didn't care one way or the other. He was still gorgeous and everything he wanted. Caleb snuffled into the back of Ian's neck.

"Did Terra come home?"

"No." Ian's shoulders bunched. "I brought him home."

No apologies. No excuses. That wasn't Ian's way. Caleb rested his lips against Ian's skin. He stood stiff, anxious, in Caleb's arms.

"Why?" Caleb brushed tender lips to the underside of Ian's ear.

"Remember that morning you brought me Terra?"

Caleb paused his nibbling. "How could I forget?" That was the day Caleb's life changed irrevocably for the better. Terra had been kicked out of her mother's home by her mother's then boyfriend. In the dead of winter. After he'd tried to rape her. She'd been all of fourteen. Better? Yes. Easy? Of course not. A lot of heartache that winter, but it gave all three of them, Ian, Caleb, and Terra, a family.

"I saw..." Ian swallowed. His hands fisted around the dishcloth in his hand. His shoulders clenched and rippled as he struggled inside with something that Caleb couldn't see. "He hadn't tripped. He'd almost passed out."

"Babe," Caleb murmured against his neck. He encircled his waist a little tighter.

"Are you mad?"

"Not really. Wasn't expecting to have a new tenant when I got home." Caleb realized he really wasn't that upset. He'd seen the boy but hadn't *seen* him. If Ian felt this way, there was a reason.

He worked Ian's death grip loose from the cloth until it fell to the sink basin, urging him tenderly to turn around. "You do know what you're getting into, right?"

"Of course not." Ian huffed, then lowered his head to rest against Caleb's shoulder.

"There's a good chance it will blow up in your face," Caleb cautioned. "Not everyone lost wants to be found."

"I know that, too. I've seen those kids at the shelter. They're in for a day, maybe two, then they're gone again."

"So why this one?" Caleb caressed the nape of Ian's neck with caring brushes of his fingertips. Ian had never done anything like this before.

"Honestly..." Ian burrowed against Caleb. "I couldn't walk away. Grint left, then you went back to work, and I..." He cleared his throat, finally wrapping around Caleb in return, looking for strength, giving as much as taking. "I couldn't move."

"Then you did the right thing, babe," he said gently. "You did the right thing."

* * * *

Parker grimaced at the mess of clothes he had. Everything was filthy. After scrubbing for half an hour to get through the layers of dirt, he really didn't want to put them back on, but knew he didn't have a choice.

Finally choosing the least worn pieces he had, he dressed. He didn't know if he would be out in ten minutes, in the morning, or next week, so he left everything else in the pack.

Cautiously opening the door, he listened. There was the quietest rumble of talking voices. The law was home. He had expected as much.

Time to see what would happen. He didn't have high hopes Caleb would be all right with Parker under the same roof. No one was that understanding.

Except when he expected fierce anger and unwelcoming scorn, he found them wrapped around one another in front of the sink. It was *not* a sight Parker was used to seeing. Grown men didn't do that. If they did, it was in the dark, behind closed doors. Behind barns. In secret.

Not that it kept Parker's father from learning the truth. He carefully touched his loose tooth with his tongue. His last reminder from his father. He'd learned his lesson. Parker hadn't spoken of it since that last beating. If his father could do that, he wasn't about to risk a stranger's opinion.

Caleb straightened and running fingers through Ian's hair, said something privately. The caring action made Parker's throat tighten. Ian pressed into the caress and nodded. They were so comfortable, so open. Parker almost felt like he was intruding. That was when Ian seemed to notice him standing by the kitchen wall. He eased away from Caleb's hold, but only to let him turn in Parker's direction.

"Parker, I'd like you to meet Caleb."

Parker drew a steadying breath and moved forward. He offered a hand. "Thank you for your hospitality."

"Got good manners, son. Glad to meet you." He shook then studied him. "You need clean clothes." He faced Ian. "Do we have anything that will fit him?"

"I think the boys may have left some stuff behind," Ian answered. "I'll look in Terra's closet." Ian walked from the kitchen, leaving him alone with Caleb.

Boys?

"Parker. Any last name?"

Parker bristled. Why did they always ask? "I'm not wanted." Man, these two were tall *and* nosy. Parker was only five-ten. He had to look up to both of them. If he'd been at riding weight, he'd be more compact but he'd lost weight over the last three years, making him no match at all for either of these two.

"Didn't ask if you were." Caleb rested against the sink, crossing his arms. Parker knew that stare. He was being examined, judged. "That accent..."

"Texas, sir." He reached for his hat, remembering too late he hadn't put it on.

The move made Caleb's lips twitch at the corner. "I know the feeling. You feel naked without it."

"Yes," he replied.

"So, just give me the particulars."

Parker stuck his fingers into his pockets. No sense in playing stupid with the law. "Twenty. Kicked out right before my seventeenth birthday. Been moving ever since. Had a job after school but that's been it."

"Why?"

"He caught me kissing my best friend in the horse stall."

"I take it your best friend wasn't a girl?"

"No, sir."

"Did he punch on you before that?"

Parker shrugged. "Some."

Caleb didn't seem to like that answer. His eyes grew stormy. "Well, no one will here. And no one will care who you kiss."

It was about then that Ian reappeared. He had a fistful of clothing. "This is Jenson's stuff. He won't miss it. It's been here for almost a year as it is."

"Jenson?" He didn't want to take another person's clothing.

"My nephew," Caleb explained.

"See if it fits. I'll take you tomorrow to the thrift store for work clothes and the store for a couple of extra good pieces."

"I can't pay for that." Parker hadn't accepted the thrust ball of clothes, yet, either.

"You won't. You'll work for it. Just like we talked about." Ian tapped his chest with the clothes. "He won't miss them. Grab your other stuff and you can run it through the washer by itself."

When Parker still hesitated, Ian said, "There's nothing to be ashamed of. You have what you have, and that's okay." Another nudge. "Go on."

Parker's throat worked, and a hand rose. "Thank you." The clothes found their way into his hand.

"Scoot," Caleb said, tipping his head in prompt.

"Yes, sir." Parker hopped on his toes and rushed for the bedroom they'd given him.

Closing the door, he panted, confused, and unsure, but safe. At least for right now.

He changed quickly, dumping his wallet, the twenty he'd saved from his pocket, and the small pocketknife he carried, into his boot. With his entire wardrobe wadded up into his hands, he walked out to the kitchen again.

He found Caleb getting something to drink out of the fridge. A door opened to the side of the kitchen. "In here."

Parker strode to Ian, spotting the washer behind him. "Wanted to make sure I'd remembered to empty the dryer."

"He's terrible at it," Caleb jabbed with a light laugh.

"Yeah, yeah." Ian grumbled. "Run them, and then you can toss them in the dryer in the morning."

Ian moved out of the way to let Parker wash his clothes. Caleb left the kitchen and a few seconds later, he heard a television turn on.

A hand found his shoulder and he flinched.

"It's okay," Ian offered, squeezing kindly before letting him go. "Relax. You're getting strung out for nothing. Wait until you meet the kids, then you'll *want* to run for the hills." Ian chuckled kindly.

"Kids?"

"Yeah. They're about your age. Nephews." Ian's eyes widened. "Shit! I forgot about Terra. Go ahead. We'll be in front of the TV." Then he was gone.

Parker dumped everything he held in the basin, added soap, closed it up and turned the knob. It started to hum. He hoped it was safe and he didn't accidentally, magically, break it.

Leaving the washroom, he found the two men smiling and holding hands, sitting side by side on the couch. He guessed the proposal news had been well received. Glancing around the room, he spotted a wall of pictures. Among them was a young, dark-haired girl. Well, if you didn't count the neon pink in her hair, anyway. She stood with Ian holding fishing poles while he held a stringer of fish. "Is that Terra?"

"That's her." Caleb stood. He pointed out another photo. "And this menace is my nephew, now her fiancé," he said with pride.

"You're kidding?"

"Nope." He rose up two frames. "This is my older brother and his wife, and all three boys. Aaron, Jenson, Blake. And this cutie is our goddaughter, Summer." A child sitting on top of a pony was smiling like she'd won the lottery.

"Wow." He studied more of the pictures. "And these two? He looks like you."

"That's Jake, and the blond holding the trophy is Brice, his husband. He'd won first place in one of those festival vegetable things. And this young lady is Rebecca, Jake's girl."

Parker took in all the photos. "That's a lot of family."

"They're a handful." He returned to the couch to sit with Ian.

Parker yawned. The long day, food, and shower were catching up to him. Not to mention all the shocks of the unknown and stress. He was beat.

"You don't have to wait for us. I'll wake you in the morning for breakfast then we'll get you a few things," Ian told him.

"You're sure?" He asked because he really needed to know. He couldn't completely hide his trepidation.

"You'll need something for work on Monday. Believe me, I will put you to work."

Accepting Ian's advice, he went down the hall for the bedroom they'd given him. Stripping down to nothing with everything in the washer, he huddled under the soft blankets.

Knowing a little more than he had a few hours before, he could see the room had once belonged to a girl. There were pictures of guys glued around the mirror, a big, stuffed pink dog hung out in a corner, and around the dog's neck was a graduation sash.

Closing his eyes, he blew out a breath, wanting to let it all go to relax. At least for tonight. It had been a good, long time since he'd had a bed without earning it in some way. He wanted to enjoy tonight's sleep. He couldn't swear it wouldn't be the last for a while.

Chapter Four

Parker blinked blearily when there was a knock on the bedroom door. "Parker? Food in twenty."

He licked his lips and managed a croaked, "Okay." He plopped onto the pillow, stretching limbs in slow increments. He must have slept like the dead. He didn't think he'd moved at all from how he'd fallen asleep.

He dressed and shuffled to the bathroom, still trying to wake up. He discovered a small stack of personal items on the commode tank. From a razor to a toothbrush and everything else he needed. It hadn't been there the night before. It left him stunned and unmoving for a few minutes. These two men, whom he hadn't known barely twelve hours ago, were being kinder than his own father had ever been.

Parker had always lived in his father's shadow. It was hard to be anything more than Chet Vandersoot's son when his father was around. And he'd never lived up to the old man's legend, or expectations.

Using the bathroom, he felt more human and far more awake when he was done. He scrubbed his head with stiff fingernails, aware he needed a haircut. At least he hadn't caught anything crawly. The idea of it made him shudder. Being clean all by itself was heaven.

He joined Ian and Caleb in the kitchen. "If you want, the coffee is there." Ian pointed to the filling carafe.

A knock at the door didn't seem to startle either man. Caleb went to answer the door.

"I'm going to switch my clothes."

"Okay." Ian didn't look twice. Plates were stacked high with food on the counter. It seemed like a lot, but what did he know? Parker couldn't take it all in that early in the morning.

Parker took care of his clothes, starting them to dry. When he came out, he almost bumped into Caleb holding the young girl from the photos.

"Who's that?" She pointed right at Parker.

"It's not polite to point," Caleb corrected her, drawing her hand down gently. "This is Parker. He's staying with us for a little while."

She gave him a bold stare then stretched out for him, leaping from Caleb's hold. "Catch me!"

Parker did, barely.

"Summer!" a woman cried.

"I got her," Parker offered, wrapping her up close. Small arms cinched around his neck. She wasn't going anywhere.

"This is Jeannie and Wanda." Caleb made the introductions.

Parker blinked. He immediately got the impression they *weren't* sisters. "Nice to meet you," he said, remembering to at least try to smile. It had been so long since he'd been with a crowd, and just him and his father in a room were *not* a crowd. They usually barely talked.

"I guess I should have warned you. We all do breakfast on Sunday, and this is our weekend." Ian shrugged a shoulder, like it wasn't any big deal.

Summer ran fingers through his hair. "This is like Mama's."

He noticed one of the ladies had brown hair like his, to the shoulders.

"Wanda, help me with the table. Tucker's coming with Vivian." Caleb pulled on the table, and the woman helped him put a leaf in it.

"It's a mad house, isn't it?" Jeannie said.

"Is she always this friendly?" he asked, watching Summer as she settled against his shoulder.

"Yes and no. With family, try and stop her. Out in the big, wide world? Not so much."

"Door!" Summer cried when someone knocked.

"I'll go," Jeannie offered, tapping Summer on the nose before she left.

More people piled into the house. He recognized Caleb's brother and his blond husband. Then another blond and he guessed his wife.

Everyone said hi to him and to Summer. He shook hands when he dared.

"She's not too heavy, is she? She doesn't realize she's not a baby any longer," Wanda said.

"She's fine." He caught it when Summer snuggled up against his neck. He blinked at her friendly innocence.

"I like you," she whispered.

"Tell you a secret," he said as quietly. Her eyes grew wide in excitement. "I like you, too."

"Is this everyone?" Caleb called.

"Think so."

"Looks like it."

"Good! Grab a plate and a chair." Caleb and Ian got out of the way as everyone lined up and went down the counter, stacking their plates with food.

"What do you want?" Parker asked the munchkin in his arms.

"Toast, fries, and a little egg, please," she said as sweetly as any child he'd ever heard.

"Fries?"

"She means the hash browns," the person behind him explained.

Parker managed to balance her and a plate, settling her in a chair next to one of her moms.

"Thank you," Jeannie said. "Better get yours before the rest of the carnivores eat it all." She began to butter Summer's toast.

With a plate in hand, he faced the table, and suddenly realized he was in a house full of people he didn't know.

"Here." One of the blond men smiled and patted the chair next to him. "Welcome to the family."

"Thank you," he managed, easing into the chair carefully to not tap anyone. It wasn't too overwhelming with Summer on his other side.

"I'm Brice." He offered a hand.

He gave his name with the handshake. "Is this normal?" he asked at Brice's shoulder.

"No, usually there's water guns, banshee screams, and cake involved."

"What?" he chirped, leaning away, hunting for escape routes.

"Quit scaring him, Brice," Ian chided. "He's working for me starting tomorrow."

Caleb stood and the louder chatter fell off. "Since this is the best chance with so many of us together. Terra called last night."

Brice bounced in his chair a little, apparently happy about the coming announcement.

"Aaron took the plunge. He asked her yesterday."

A cheer that rocked the windows filled the home.

Caleb's brother on Brice's other side raised his orange juice. "To Terra and Aaron."

It was followed with another loud cheer and even a happy clapping from Summer.

Talk soon fell into loops of the newly engaged, Brice's garden, jobs, and normal things.

Parker ate quietly, absorbing what he could, listening. He ate far slower than the night before, aware now his tooth wasn't going to take much punishment. It helped that he wasn't starving, not feeling like a deep breath would let him count his spinal divots from the inside.

"Where are you from?" Brice asked.

He took a drink of juice to clear his throat. "Galveston."

Brice turned to his husband. "Told you. You owe me five bucks."

"What?" Parker arched an eyebrow.

"I said Texas. He said Oklahoma." He winked. "I'm from West Virginia so everyone sounds funny to me." He poured the accent on thick, making Parker laugh because it sounded like *Wes' Vaginnya*. "What do you do?"

"Do?"

"Are you a mechanic?" He waved his fork toward Ian, then snagged a sausage on the end. "You're working for him, right?"

"Well, I will be." Though he really had no idea what that entailed. "But no, not a mechanic." He pushed food around. "I was a bull rider on the junior circuit. I've worked with horses my whole life."

"Horsey!" Summer cried, munching on toast happily.

Parker smiled, feeling the wistful loss. "Yeah. Those big brutes." He reached and tickled her tummy on his other side, having her dissolve into a fit of giggles. Maybe someday he'd at least get to own one again. He missed riding his gelding, Chaser.

"Did you ever reach Champion level?"

"No. That takes years and I had to quit."

"Hey, the fall rodeo is right around the corner, isn't it?" someone offered.

"Yeah, the weekend before teacher in-service starts."

Caleb smirked. "Which is worse, Brice? Riding a two-thousand pound keg of dynamite, or a senior class?"

He held up a finger, his mouth popping open. Then he snorted. "I concede that one. My classes have been very good."

Gradually, everyone finished and soon they started to leave, until it was just Brice, Jake, and Summer's little family.

"Who does the dishes?" Parker was avoiding the kitchen right then, and trying to not look like he was.

"The house that cooked last weekend, cleans this weekend, etc," Jeannie said. "Which means it's our turn."

"So one house cooks, another picks up?"

"Pretty much," Wanda offered. Somehow in the moving and juggling, Parker had ended up on the couch with Summer snuggled on his lap. "It really doesn't take long this way, and no one is exhausted after a hoard like ours." She flipped loose strands out of Summer's face. "Well, almost no one."

"She really is sweet," he said, rubbing her back as she snoozed.

"Let me go lend a hand before they come hunting for me."

He smiled for Wanda. "We'll be fine." He guessed he was still waiting for the shoe to drop for all the kindness. His head was spinning from all the people this morning. He'd lost track at one point and hoped no one really noticed. Thankfully, maybe even more so, they hadn't poked too hard at him with questions.

Maybe he was far enough away from Galveston that his father's name wouldn't mean anything.

It felt good to relax in comfort and anonymity. A bed last night, two hot meals in a row, and a shower. He rested on the couch himself until he heard voices getting closer.

Parker let his hands glide free of his cuddler when someone lifted a drowsy and limp Summer off his lap. She sank her head to Ian's shoulder. "Be right back, then we'll head out."

He stretched his arms over his head, groaning as he did.

After standing, he went to the bedroom and pulled on his boots, meeting up with Ian again in the living room. Jake was helping Caleb put the table back to its normal size.

"Okay, see you guys later." When they were done, Jake and Brice hugged and waved then left.

Ian smooched on Caleb and then ushered Parker outside.

"This won't take long. I hate shopping."

Parker snickered, climbing into the truck. That was one thing they could agree on then.

* * * *

Ian introduced Parker to Jackson and Brock the next morning. "Make sure if you ask him for a hand, you explain it. He's never worked in an auto shop and what you know like the toss of a hat, he may not."

"I'm not dumb," Parker snapped.

"Do you know an oil filter from a gas filter?" Ian asked without pressure.

Parker's eyes clouded.

He didn't push when he knew he'd made his point. "Don't worry. You'll catch on quick. I'll show you what I want cleaned around the bays, and as you get more comfortable, we'll show you how to do tire repair and hands-on jobs. I also want you to answer the phone when it rings. There's the one in the main office, and the one hanging up over there." He pointed to a side wall.

He'd already filled out the necessary paperwork, so the kid was ready to start. Ian spent the morning showing him the cleaning bins, the collection containers, and waste containers that required locks and why.

"And this is all regulated?"

"Down to the ants on the barrel, practically," he said, only mildly joking. "So it might look like pointless crap, but too much of this unaccounted for, and I'm out of business and all my licensing. Just so you don't think I've given you some shit job, which it is, but it's still important."

Parker huffed, but grinned. "I get it."

"Now I believe you when you say you're not dumb."

And that was where Ian had left him two hours ago, working on checking and cross-checking various containers and waste logs.

"Doing okay?" Ian asked, wiping his hands on a rag as he neared. "You ready for something else?"

Parker checked numbers against the computer screen in front of him. "This is the last one."

"Good." He waited for Parker to finish then blanked the screen on the system. He frowned when Parker turned around. "Is your jaw hurting you?"

Parker shrugged. "It's been achy since last night. Why?"

"Because it's swollen."

Parker lifted a hand and hunted for the growing lump under his jaw. His eyes widened when he winced in pain. "Okay, now that hurts."

"Let's get you over to the dental office and see if they can get you in."

"I can't afford that."

"And I'm not going to let you avoid it." He strode into the inner bay before the boy could argue more. "Jackson! I have to run an errand with Parker. You and Brock hold it down until I get back."

"Everything okay?" He popped out of the engine he was working on. "Oh, shit. Dude. Your face."

Parker grimaced. "That's what I hear."

Ian unzipped his overalls and dropped them over a tool bin. "If I can't get right back, I'll call." He didn't give Parker a chance to fight about it. "Unzip, now."

Parker did, albeit grudgingly.

Chapter Five

"Is Doc Kirkpatrick available?"

Will stopped at the corner of the hallway, taking in the pair at the counter. He was pretty sure he recognized the mechanic from the shop across town. The younger man was a stranger to him. He'd only been in Jasper since early spring, so knowing anyone outside of the office wasn't likely.

"Sorry, Dr. Kirkpatrick isn't here. Dr. Parkinson is, though."

"Can he see someone?" Will saw him tug the younger man to the counter. "He has an infected, loose tooth."

"It's okay, Tammie. I'll have to count the eleven as a cancellation." This definitely wasn't Linda Hampstead. He waved to the young man. "I can see him."

"I'll wait here, Parker."

Pleading eyes sought the other man. "Ian."

"No arguments."

Parker, apparently, sighed. "I hate dentists," he grumbled.

"I hear that all the time," Will murmured. "Tammie, prep the X-ray, please."

He heard Tammie handing over the required papers for information as he sat Parker into the exam chair in an offset room. He slipped on latex gloves, then clipped a paper bib around his neck. "Parker, right?"

"Yes."

"Let me just take a quick look then we'll take an X-ray to see how deep the damage is."

Parker grunted. He'd closed his eyes in avoidance.

Will frowned at the care of his teeth. "You need a good cleaning, and need to make very personal friends with your buddy, dental floss."

Parker scrunched his nose, though with a depressor in his mouth, he wasn't trying to talk.

"X-ray is warmed up and loaded."

"Thank you, Tammie," he said loud enough to be heard over his shoulder. He tossed the wood in the trash bin, then unclipped the younger man. "Let's go." He moved out of the way and guided him into the hall. "Chin on the cup." He aligned the panorama X-ray. "Stay as still as you can." When that was done, he took him back to the chair. "I want to do panels on the bad side. Can you clench your teeth enough to hold the frame?"

"I think so."

Will prepped him with the lead chest blanket then told him to stay still, positioning the large, mobile X-ray against his jaw. A snap and a whir and it was done.

"Okay. Hang tight while I get these developed."

"I can't pay for this. I'm already in debt to Ian."

Will patted his arm. "We'll figure out something."

Parker huffed, looking away out the side window to the dusty parking lot.

"Going to owe half the town in a week," Will heard in a cross mutter.

Once the images were done, he carried them to the room and pinned them on the light board. He lowered to the rolling stool to make room for his patient. "The news isn't good, but I think we can save what's around it."

Parker sat up on the seat, following Will's explanation.

"This one will have to come out. It's cracked below the gum line, but if we can get all the infection, you shouldn't have any root damage on either of these two." He tapped the glowing white shapes.

"So I have to have it pulled?"

"Sorry, yes."

Parker sank to lean on his knees in grumbled defeat. "Shoulda just kept walking."

"When can you come in for the full work?"

"I don't know. Let me check with my boss."

"I'll also prescribe an antibiotic you need to take for three days prior to the extraction. It will reduce the swelling and make it easier on you until the antibiotics are full strength in your system."

"Lovely," he retorted. "Fine." He found his feet. "Am I done?"

Will met his tired eyes. "For now, yes."

"Thanks." He almost ran from the room.

Will followed him to the counter and wrote out the prescription. "He'll need this." He handed it to the older man. He could be his step-father, Will supposed. He'd called him by name. "When can he come in for the extraction?"

"How long will you need?"

"An hour should be good. He'll be down for the afternoon, but on his feet by the next day provided he isn't suffering any repercussions. If you want him in as soon as possible, with this..." He handed over the prescription. "Thursday."

"Ian," Parker pleaded.

"Earliest on Thursday." Ian wasn't making any bones about getting this done.

Parker threw up his hands and stormed out of the office.

"Will you be here or Dr. Kirkpatrick?"

"I will be." John hadn't made a formal announcement that he was retiring, so he'd been telling everyone he was simply there helping out. If he wasn't considered a permanent interloper, it gave the town a chance to get used to seeing him, a chance to make a foothold in what would roll into his own practice sometime in the next six months.

Ian shook his hand. "Thanks for seeing him. I'll have him here."

"Make sure he takes those. He's already got an infection building."

"What can he do about the swelling?" He folded the script and stuffed it in a rear pocket.

"Ice packs, and nothing hard or crunchy. It's cracked, so any extra pressure will irritate the root."

"I'll let him know. Thanks again."

Will saw him and Parker get into an old truck and leave the parking lot out front.

"It's a shame he's married," Tammie said wistfully to the empty room.

"Parker?"

"No!" She smacked his side and laughed. "Ian. Parker is too young for me." She pulled up his paperwork. "Says he's twenty. Almost twenty-one. I'm not a cougar."

Will shook his head, swallowing his chuckles. "Bad, Tammie."

"Besides, Ian's safe to like from a distance. He's gay."

Will started to stand then did a double take. "But you just said he was married."

She began straightening Parker's file. "For a while now. Um... One of the Sheriffs." Her brow tightened as she tried to remember then she snapped her fingers. "Drew! Sheriff Drew is his honey."

"And that doesn't bother you?" He managed to keep his mouth from hitting the desk. Just.

Tammie's lips thinned and with Parker's file in hand, she stood and faced him. "If you have a problem with it, you better find a new practice, Dr. Parkinson. Jasper doesn't judge people like that."

"Whoa!" He held up a hand. "It just surprised me at how easily you accept it."

"What's to accept?" She rolled a shoulder and then sauntered past him.

"Huh," he said when she was gone. He seriously doubted that would be the last time he'd be put in his place by his tech assistant.

He also wondered how welcoming the town would be if they knew their newest dentist was just like Ian.

* * * *

By Thursday, Parker was in misery and ready to have his tooth removed—via beheading.

Ian and Caleb had both been understanding, while he'd been so miserable, he'd wanted to cry in his sleep. He knew he'd been an ass more than once, but they hadn't taken it personally. He'd tried to work, and had been relocated to the office to answer the phone. The tooth had started to give him a headache on Tuesday, and by Thursday, he knew his head was going to explode.

He didn't put up a single ounce of fight when Ian said it was time for his appointment. He would have driven himself if he could see straight.

"He's in good hands," Dr. Parkinson said before he led Parker to the room. "I'll have Tammie call you to come get him when he's able."

Parker practically crawled into the curved chair. "Never thought I'd want to see this room again."

The dentist smiled, flashing brilliant white and straight teeth. *He would have a great smile.*

"Don't worry. We'll numb you up to your eyeballs. You won't feel a thing."

"Make it so I don't feel a thing for the next four days, and you have a deal." Parker guessed he was due some pain-free days.

Dr. Parkinson chuckled. "Can't make that promise, but I promise to do it fast and make it easy on you." He patted Parker's arm. "Okay, relax."

Parker nodded and mumbled in the appropriate places, cringing when certain sounds were just *too* clear. He sighed in relief when he knew the worst was over.

"Almost done."

Point proven. Groggily, he stared at the intense gray gaze working over him. A breathing mask covered half his face, so all Parker really had to focus on was his eyes. Parker didn't think he was very old. He *acted* older and patient, but looked young. His hands were steady. His wishes were crisp to Tammie, confident, the voice even and unhurried. He had straight brown hair, dark, like a beaver's pelt. Darker than Parker's. Professional short. Handsome. Maybe a touch of what could even be called rugged.

"Okay," he said, breaking into Parker's ruminating. "Let's rinse." He sat straight at Parker's shoulder as Tammie took care of that. Parker was glad they were almost done. His jaw was starting to ache for a different reason now. "I mean what I said. You need a thorough, deep cleaning."

"That's what happens when you're homeless for three years," he mumbled. He really didn't know why he said that, but he couldn't take back the truth. Though he supposed by now, it was closer to four. He hadn't been keeping that kind of track.

Dr. Parkinson's eyes widened for a heartbeat. "Well, I'm glad you're here now." He leaned close. "Okay, last check and then we'll get you out of here. Relax."

Parker closed his eyes, letting him do his final round of poking.

* * * *

Will was used to getting all kinds of excuses for laziness. He hadn't heard that one before. He also realized it wasn't an excuse.

Almost twenty-one. Homeless for three years. Those two sentences played on a loop through his mind as he finished removing all the needed protection from around Parker. He patted his shoulder. "Stay put. Tammie will call Ian for you."

Parker raised a hand and touched his arm when they were alone. "Thank you. For not making it hurt. Hated my dentist at home. He didn't like kids."

"Then why go to him?"

"He didn't hate my dad."

Will nodded in understanding. "Ahh. Money, huh?"

Parker seemed to struggle for a minute, deciding what to say. "He's well-known in Galveston. People worship him."

Parker's hand fell loosely and he closed his eyes. Will took that as he wasn't going to add to it.

"Just rest for now. You'll need to take it easy for the next twelve hours or so. Nothing iced, or super hot." When Parker wasn't responding, he added, "I'll tell Ian and make sure he has your care instructions."

"Good idea," Parker said. "How soon before I'm not numb? I can't feel my lips."

Will smiled at his expressions as he tried to feel them. "It won't be long, less than an hour probably."

"Will it hurt, then?" he asked warily.

"Shouldn't. If it does, call me."

Parker settled into the chair. "I'm taking your word."

"My word is good, Parker."

Will made himself stand up from his stool and walk out of the room before he let simple ramblings turn into something he didn't want to deal with.

Chapter Six

Ian followed him inside until he'd eased himself lightly to the couch. "Sleep it off. I'll be home in a few hours. Your prescriptions should be ready then."

"Yay," he groaned, sure he sounded as pathetic as he felt.

Ian squeezed his shoulder and then he was gone.

Parker slept while he could. He tried not to think about the bill he was going to see from Dr. Parkinson. Without insurance, he was sure it was going to be something with a comma in it.

Agitation compounded with worry skewed his dreams. The scent of sun-warmed hay and clean horse filled his memories as he drifted. The clip of iron on concrete as horses stamped their feet. He'd spent many hours in the barn, and a few in the hayloft when he just wanted to get away from his dad and life. The days he'd spent riding were some of his best memories.

Then there was *that* day. The day he'd kissed Travis. The day his life went to shit.

He could see his dad walking toward him in his mental vision. He tried to hide Travis behind him. The boy's shirt was unbuttoned. He could still remember the warmth of skin beneath his palms, the heady beat of Travis' heart behind exposed ribs. They were supposed to be cleaning out Chaser's stall. Well, they had been. Until Travis had slid a palm inside Parker's rear pocket to cup his butt with a firm grip.

They found themselves pressed together, pinned into a corner of the stall.

"Didn't know you felt this way," Travis said, hoarse and trembling with nervous energy.

"That I'd rather touch a guy?" he asked, nuzzling at Travis' chin. Excitement coursed through his body.

Travis moaned. "I was going to play it off as a joke if you didn't...weren't..." He shivered. "Been wantin' to kiss you for two years."

Crisp blue eyes poked through Parker's hesitations and he dove for his best friend's shirt. Travis jumped then lurched for Parker's mouth. It was hot and sloppy and more than he'd ever felt in his life.

Travis was a little older than Parker's almost seventeen, but they'd been riding and playing since the third grade. Parker didn't know where to begin, running his hands up and down Travis' chest. Hot skin burned, making him hungry and needy for more.

Travis had knocked Parker's hat off his head, digging demanding fingers into his hair as the kiss grew heated.

He hadn't heard the side door and almost missed the slap of his dad's boots. He pushed Travis away and whirled, keeping the other boy behind him.

Travis was solid, and could probably take Chet in a sound and fair fight, but this was Parker's dad, and he'd be damned before he'd let his old man lay a finger on his best friend.

He didn't have anything to worry about.

Chet's swing wasn't aimed at Travis at all.

"God damn fucking faggot!"

His fist found Parker's jaw with the force of a jackhammer. It would be months before the crack that hit caused made itself known. He was on the ground, curling into a ball before the full impact of the fist had registered.

The toe of his father's boot caught Parker in his ribs when he tried to roll away.

Travis jumped his dad and pulled him off Parker.

"Get off my property! Now!" he screamed when he managed to jerk Travis off his back.

Travis' self-preservation won. He dashed out of the barn like his heels were on fire.

That was the last time he saw his best friend.

It was the last time Parker saw any of his life.

* * * *

He popped awake and scrambled away from the face staring down at him.

"Easy, son." Caleb's expression was worried. "You were dreaming."

Parker scrubbed a palm over his face, noticing he could feel it right before the ache of his jaw reminded him why he had been asleep to begin with and that he shouldn't be pushing on his face like that.

"You okay?"

Out of sorts and confused, he nodded. "Yeah." He really had no idea what okay was any longer.

"I'm going to work. If you need anything, call Ian at the shop. The number's by the phone. He'll get what you need on the way home."

"I'll be okay." He sagged to rest his head on the armrest of the couch.

Caleb straightened and started to leave.

"Caleb?"

He paused, his hand on the door.

"Do you mind if I make a call?"

"Go ahead. Though, if you call your dad, neither I nor Ian will let that man hurt you. That is over." Caleb said that with smooth authority.

Parker believed him.

"Not Dad," he said.

"Okay. Take it easy this afternoon."

Caleb left.

Hefting himself up to his feet, he made his feet take him to the kitchen. With something to write on, he called information and made sure he knew the number. His heart was jumping like a herd of five year-olds on a trampoline as he punched the numbers.

"Hello?" The voice was rough. Parker thought it was Travis' dad.

He licked his lips, feeling how dry they were. "Is Travis there?"

"Parker?" Sheer shock made the voice on the other end warble. It was Travis, but he sounded so graveled.

He sagged against the refrigerator, stunned and overwhelmed all at once to hear his friend's voice, *any* friend's voice, after so long. "Yeah. It's me."

"Holy shit. You're alive!"

He snorted, staying the sniffle before it became obvious. He'd never expected his friend to be happy to hear from him. Not after that day in the barn. He'd almost gotten Travis murdered. "He didn't kill me."

"Damn. I thought he had. You just vanished."

"He kicked me out after..." All he'd had was the wallet in his pocket, and the clothes on his back. He'd threatened Parker with physical harm, the police, anything he could think of. Chet had gone so far as threatening Travis and his family. Parker refused to bring any of that anger down on Travis or anyone else.

"Where are you?"

"Iowa."

"Are you coming home?"

Parker sighed at his friend's hopeful excitement. "No. I'm never coming back, Travis." Galveston was Chet's town, not home. Not anymore. He refused to be a minion, a son by name only, and one that wasn't even wanted. "Why do you sound like your old man?" He had no interest in asking about his own.

"I got hit in the throat going over horns."

"Where was your collar?" he asked with rushed shock. Parker knew Travis wouldn't have ridden without it.

Travis grew quiet. "All I had was my vest and helmet. That was the day my dad found out I was gay. We had a big fight and I wasn't in my head. He had a heart attack that night."

"Fuck. I'm sorry."

"Nothing you did. Then or ever," he replied honestly. "Man, I can't believe you called. Iowa, right?"

"Yeah."

"Hey, how close are you to Jasper? There's a PBR string going through there on its way north and I'm riding."

"No shit?"

"Can you be there?"

Parker looked out the kitchen window, shaking his head at pure dumb luck and coincidence. "Yeah, I can be there. Won't be riding. Been too long."

"Fuck! I don't care. It'll be good to just see you."

Parker smiled. "You too." He swallowed, feeling his throat tighten. "I've missed you."

"Missed you, too." He breathed shakily. "Okay, I'm getting off the phone before I start bawling like a broad."

Same ol' Travis. "See you in a few weeks. I'll look for you."

"I'll be on the road by the weekend, so call before if it changes."

"Ride safe," he said, the same thing he'd always told his best friend before a ride.

"I will."

They hung up and for the first time in years, Parker felt light.

The next few days fell into a pattern. He worked with Ian at the shop, started to get a handle on the underbelly of a mechanic's life, and discovered he liked having something to do every day, somewhere to go. Somewhere he was wanted.

Sunday breakfast was at Jake and Brice's, where he discovered Jake made killer pancakes. Summer became his shadow just like the previous Sunday, and he found himself smiling and actually laughing again.

They were sitting around the table, already deep into all sorts of discussions when someone knocked on Jake's door.

"We're all here, right?" Jake asked.

"Doesn't look like anyone's missing," Caleb replied.

Jake shook his head in confusion and left the table to answer the door.

"Are we too late for food?" A young woman appeared, with a guy in tow talking to Jake. Parker recognized both and wasn't surprised by the shouts of welcome.

Sitting beside Brice again to eat this weekend, Parker noticed the blond was trying to hide his broad smiles. "You knew, didn't you?"

"Yup," he said under his breath. He leaned close. "She called last night and warned me. I just didn't let the cat out of the bag."

Parker chuckled with him as Ian hugged on Terra and she and Aaron hugged on everyone. Somehow, Summer crawled onto his lap to make room for the two new arrivals, and they wound up eating and being silly together.

"You've been adopted," Brice warned with humor.

"I don't mind being a big brother." He shrugged. Summer was too sweet for her own good. Precocious. And he knew she'd be trouble with a capital T in about a dozen years.

Summer tipped to stare at him upside down. Then she tugged on Wanda's sleeve beside them. "Mama? I want Parker to be my big brother. Can we keep him?"

Parker felt his face heat like a furnace. He didn't realize she'd understand what that meant. Brice's quiet snicker at his shoulder wasn't helping him any.

"If he doesn't mind having a squirt for his baby sister." Wanda winked at him.

Summer twisted to regard Parker. "You don't mind, right? I can be your sister?"

He cuddled her a little closer in a hug and she giggled. "Sure, baby girl. I'll be your big brother."

She nodded once, firmly. It was a done deal.

Parker smiled and they play dueled with sausage links until he gobbled hers all the way down to her fingers, making her squeal and laugh loudly.

"You ever want to babysit, she's yours," Wanda said at his side. "She might even listen to you. For about ten minutes."

"I'll remember that." He smiled and helped Summer finish her breakfast.

Letting Summer pick at her breakfast, he got a good look at everyone at the table. Some were related by blood, others by marriage, and yet, together they made one of the largest families Parker had ever been exposed to. And almost all of them were gay.

He knew now that Brice and Tucker were brothers, that Terra was Ian's only niece, and that Summer was the only child. She was doted on but not spoiled. Wanda and Jeannie were together and owned the bakery down the walk from Lucy's where he'd first met Ian and Caleb.

He was still learning about everyone else in increments.

"Oh, when is the rodeo?" he remembered to ask.

"Next weekend." Brice put on a suffering expression. "Then my nine months of hell begins."

Parker jostled his shoulder, chuckling with him. He bit his lip a moment later. "I didn't get to finish. Missed my senior year."

"Do you want to change that?"

He looked around the table. "I'll let you know." He still didn't know if he was going to be around long enough *to* change it. Or change anything.

"If you want, I'll help you. I've helped others get their GEDs. It's not easy, but it'll give you something you can call your own."

"What?"

"Your education." Brice gave him an even stare. "I hope you stick around, but it's not a requirement for us to help you."

"It's not?" Parker straightened on his seat. He had yet to have anyone demand payment for anything, now that he thought about it. Not Ian or Caleb for the room. The agreement he'd made with Ian to work at the shop seemed to be all he wanted. No requirements to be a part of their large, boisterous family. No one had blinked an eye or raised a complaint with him being included. Not even for the dental emergency he'd found himself in. He'd never met a family like theirs. Ever.

Brice started talking and drew his focus to him.

"We all have had things happen to us. It was our personal choices to stay, and now we have this zoo." He tipped his head toward the table to keep the conversation private between them. "One of these days, when it's not as loud as a jet engine in here, I'll tell you just how Jake and I got together. His ex-wife was a nightmare of freaky proportions," he shared in a whisper.

Parker gurgled a laugh.

"Freaky!" Summer cried.

"Nice going, Uncle Brice," Jeannie scolded from Wanda's opposite side. "We almost had her out of her powder butt phase."

"Powder butt!" she cried, sending the table into fits of laughter.

"You brought that on yourself," Ian told her, waving his fork at her, showing no shame to be laughing at them as well.

"Do I want to know?" Parker asked, almost scared to find out where it had all began.

"Probably not," Wanda muttered.

"Freaky powder butt!"

Both Wanda and Jeannie groaned and the laughter took a solid ten minutes to die down.

Chapter Seven

Caleb dropped Parker off in front of the dental office the following Tuesday. "Just call Ian when you're done."

He got out of the cop cruiser and spoke through the window. "Thanks, Caleb." Caleb drove away and Parker opened the glass door of the air-conditioned office to walk in. "Hi, Tammie."

"Morning, Parker. Go ahead and have a seat. He's finishing with someone and then he'll look at you."

Taking one of the waiting padded chairs, he reached for a magazine and absently flipped through it. *Nothing but ads.* He tossed it to the table when after eight pages, there still wasn't anything to read.

Not too long after, a heavyset woman walked from the rear and started talking to Tammie to pay.

"Parker?"

His gaze swept from the ladies to the man in the hall. A smile warmed the man's face in welcome. *Is that a dimple?* Parker hadn't paid that much attention last visit, worried about having his tooth yanked. He was pretty sure the man had dimples now that he could get a good look, but it had been so quick and fleeting, he wasn't sure he saw it or imagined it.

"Come on back."

Dutifully, he trailed Dr. Parkinson to one of the rooms. "Go ahead and have a seat. This won't take long. Just want to check that you're healing well."

Parker watched him repeat the scene from before. Gloves, bib, depressor. He found himself looking into his eyes again. He supposed it wasn't unusual. They were barely inches apart—if he turned just right, they could kiss.

"Have you had any tenderness?"

"No," he managed without moving his tongue. How dentists understood their patients was a mystery.

"It looks like it's healing fine." He sat on the chair and removed his gloves.

"So now what?"

"Start taking care of them, while you have the chance." It felt like he moved closer to Parker, but he couldn't swear to it. "I remember what you said. Three years is a long time."

When Parker expected to see disappointment or derision, all he saw in his gray eyes was empathy.

"It's hard to take care of small details when you're in that kind of situation."

"Were you ever homeless?" Parker asked, feeling the bitter bite of skepticism leak into his voice without a problem and not bothering to hide it. He definitely didn't want or need anyone's pandering.

"For a while, yes. My mother and father lost everything. We lived out of our car for over a year."

Parker gaped at the man. "You're serious?"

"Completely. We all worked to get back on our feet. Dad got a job, then Mom. I helped her clean houses until I didn't have to. I finished school, and promised myself I'd never be there again. I found something I felt passionate about and narrowed it down to a career."

Studying the man, he wondered if that's where his calm came from. He'd already faced his own private hell, had lived through fears of what came next, what could happen and go wrong. "Can I ask how old you are?"

"Twenty-nine. By the time I graduated high school, we were stable again. I could focus on my classes. I still send home a small amount to my parents every month. Whether they use it or put it away for whenever, I don't care. I will never let them or me be there again." He stood from the seat as though just realizing how personal he was being. He fiddled with a pen on the counter. "What I'm saying is, I do understand."

Parker wondered if he'd found a kindred spirit. Someone who'd been on his road and knew what he'd lived through. He also wondered how many people he told that particular story to. Was it to help him? Ian and Caleb had been upfront since the moment Ian got him into his pickup. They wanted to help. What did the man standing before him want from him? What would Parker be in debt for when all was said and done?

When Dr. Parkinson shifted as if he was ready to let Parker leave, he asked the first thing that came to his lips. "Why are you here?"

He leaned on the counter behind him, not as tense. "I'm filling in for Dr. Kirkpatrick."

"Oh." Parker slumped on the exam chair. "So you won't be staying."

"I didn't say that."

Parker lifted his gaze and locked with gray eyes. A careening zing of energy made his heart trip for several seconds until he blinked, breaking the connection.

Dr. Parkinson cleared his throat. "If you want to make an appointment for a full cleaning, just let Tammie know." Professional and distant again.

Parker didn't mean to, but sitting where he was in the exam room, his gaze was crotch high. Even in the loose scrubs pants, Parker could see a faint outline of what looked like very awake body parts.

Had he felt it too? That little spark that hit his chest? Parker had no idea what it meant. If he wanted to feel it again, or if he'd get to. He wasn't uneducated in sex, but looking at this man in front of him with his gray eyes and dark brown hair, talking to Parker like he mattered, this didn't feel like *that*. This felt...*different*.

He stood to his feet. "I'll make you a deal. I'll do as you ask, so long as I only see you. I trust you. The only other people I've trusted since I was sixteen are Ian and Caleb."

"I can't promise that," he deflected.

"Then I won't be back. You did what was needed. I'll pay the bill as quickly as I can." He started to turn. The man knew his business, and it meant the world to him. Parker had a feeling he'd argue.

He did.

"Okay. I know I can help you get healthy again. I'll do your care."

Parker gave him a small smile. "Thank you." And maybe he'd be able to figure out why his dentist was making his body heat and his skin feel sensitive whenever they brushed against each other.

* * * *

Will followed a few paces behind until Parker was at the front counter, then he made a direct left into John's office, partially closing the door for thinking privacy. He paced in the short space in front of the desk, his steps muted by the carpet. He couldn't believe he willingly made that promise. It was unethical for one. Regardless that Will probably would have been the only one *to* do the work, any work, on anybody, the request Parker had just made was one he shouldn't have agreed to. John would still put in hours. This was still his office until he said otherwise.

Will hadn't expected the rush of attraction with Parker sitting there, talking. He'd always maintained a professional distance with his patients, until today. He never would have told his history to anyone, ever. He never had.

Until Parker. He cursed under his breath, wondering when he'd lost his mind.

He could sense the younger man was struggling to find a foothold in life again. He needed to know he wasn't alone in his doubts and fears. Needed to know he wasn't alone in his struggles.

There was opportunity here, even in a small country town the size of Jasper. Two good men had taken him in. Parker's first week in town was rolling into two. If he were in a hurry to skip town, he'd be gone. There would have been no follow-ups, no talk about future plans. He would have taken what he could and leave. He hadn't left yet.

Will's tumbling thoughts screeched to a mind-numbing stop. Will didn't know if Parker was gay. He didn't know if Parker had felt the same thing he had, or if he was going bonkers over something that was as important as umbrella colors in the rain. Meaning, not at all.

"He's not even twenty-one, yet," he berated himself. Tammie had said almost twenty-one. He wondered how close *almost* was. Will rubbed at the bridge of his nose with pinched fingers. He twisted and rested with his butt against the smooth, rounded edged of the wood desk.

There was something about Parker that he'd tried to ignore during his previous appointments, and thought he had.

Today he hadn't been so lucky. Because today he was almost positive Parker had felt it too. That awareness had heated the very air between them. "Too young, and a patient. You're just begging for trouble." It would be a good way to lose the golden opportunity he had here. His brain was making all the right arguments. He knew he should do what was right and not think about Parker.

Not that his body was listening to his common sense side now that he'd admitted what he'd felt had been real. He was simply grateful for the looseness of his pants because the sudden needy ache he'd been hit with when he'd almost fallen into Parker's eyes had taken him completely by surprise. It wasn't gone yet, either.

Parker stood about his height, with nearly shoulder-length, brown hair with sun-bleached strands that made it golden. His eyes were a green/brown hazel mixture that reflected light like slow moving water. He'd had ample opportunity to sneak peeks the times he'd been in Will's chair.

The younger man was a wild card. He had no reason to stay in Jasper. He'd been out on his own for years, and it didn't seem to have been by his choice. He'd said it not half an hour ago. He trusted only two men. And Will.

Will knew Parker wasn't stable enough in his new situation to even think of doing more with him, and he was being foolish to be having this debate with himself. He wasn't at a place in his life where he could risk his entire livelihood on one *young* man's whims. One who didn't even know what his future was going to be in two days, much less two years.

Parker trusted him to not cause him pain, nothing more. He wasn't going to abuse that trust because of an attraction that was as random as cloud shapes.

With it settled in his mind, he circled the desk. He had other work to do until his next appointment, taking advantage of the gap since Parker hadn't needed more than a few minutes for his.

Chapter Eight

"Anything you like to eat?" Ian pushed the grocery cart, holding the list. Another one of those chores that he didn't care for, but if he wanted to eat, and he liked to do that, then he had to do the shopping.

"Stuff I don't have to shoot first," Parker quipped.

Ian paused, then hooted a short laugh. "Funny. Very funny." It was early evening so there weren't a ton of people crowding the store. He refused to come here on weekends. No one could pay him to do that.

"It really doesn't matter," Parker offered. "If I didn't eat what was on my plate, I was more than welcome to go out to the barn and shovel for another two hours before bed."

"And if you did eat?"

"Then I only had to check water and hay."

"Hmmph." He could understand a man instilling responsibility in a child, but he really doubted he would like meeting Parker's father.

The boy was starting to lose his gaunt features, filling out with better food and sleep. He cleaned up well, and wasn't a sloppy type of person. Ian was personally grateful for that. He made enough of a mess alone. A house with three grown men? Catastrophe.

"Am I working Saturday?"

"If you want to," Ian replied, checking stuff off as he managed to find what he was looking for. They hadn't settled on a schedule for Parker since he hadn't made a lot of noises about staying. He was putting his earnings back into the dentist bill less a little for himself. He'd told Ian almost immediately he wanted that covered before anything else.

"Actually, I wanted to go to the rodeo."

"That's right. You rode bulls, didn't you?"

Parker nodded. "And horses."

"Do you miss it?"

Parker bit at his lip.

Ian waited him out. They hadn't talked a whole lot about where he'd come from, what he'd been doing, who he'd been, in the week and a half he'd been with them. Old wounds took time to heal. And how long that took was up to Parker. "Grab that red box there, would you?" He pointed to what he needed.

Parker did and set it in the basket. "I miss horses and riding. I don't know if I actually miss the bulls." He walked a few minutes in silence. "I called a friend from back home on Thursday."

Ian nodded. Caleb had told him Parker had asked. Neither had heard more about it. They had to give trust to earn trust. Even though he was unsure, Parker was very respectful. He hadn't taken advantage, and he'd politely asked for almost every freedom that a normal kid would take for granted. More than likely more trained control from his father.

"The guy back home..." He stumbled over his words. "He was my best friend before that happened. He's riding on Saturday, following the PBR circuit north."

"We won't stop you, Parker, if that's what you're worried about," Ian told him gently. "Of course, you'd be leaving behind several people who already care about you."

Parker blinked at him, shock drawing out his face. "I wasn't planning on leaving."

"No, maybe not right this second, but it would pop up, and you're going to question whether you should leave or stay." Ian dropped canned vegetables in the basket. "I'm not holding anything over your head. You needed something that Caleb and I could give. A roof, a little care." He paused and looked to his side. "But now you need to ask yourself what you need next."

"What I need next?" Confusion marred his brow.

"Next. Are you looking toward your future? Next week? Next year?"

Parker looked away. "No, at least, not yet."

"You're still not sure what's going to happen here?"

Parker met his gaze. A little bit of the uncertainty Ian had seen that first evening lingered in his eyes yet. "Yeah, I guess so."

Ian nodded once at his honesty and started walking again. "Well, I can tell you Caleb didn't kill either of us for bringing you home that day. So that's good."

Ian cupped his chin as though in thought to hide his smile when Parker snickered.

"Caleb's a softy."

"Don't say that where he can hear you." Ian looked behind his shoulder. "But you're right." He nudged Parker with an elbow. "Those spaghetti noodles. The angel hair." Parker grabbed them. "Thanks." He checked the list and moved again, an unhurried stroll. "So, you have a roof, a job, you're earning money. If you were to make the next decision, what would it be?"

Parker stuck fingers into his pockets and bowed his head at Ian's side, considering if he had to take a guess.

"Well, Brice said he'd help me get my GED, and I really could use a driver's license."

"Those are both things you can do here. I can tell you this, you won't get anywhere without at least your GED. I wanted to be a mechanic. My first repair was a motorcycle." He winked at Parker. "I was ten."

"No way!"

"Dad almost ripped me apart for scattering motor parts all over my bedroom, but yeah. If I wanted something else, I would still need the school for it. That goes for any job above labor."

"It's daunting," Parker said.

"It is. So is getting on the back of eighteen hundred pounds of pure adrenaline."

"I'm behind," he lamented.

"No. You're right here. There is no behind in life. There's being behind in bills, behind a slow driver, never behind in life."

"Philosophical bullshit."

"Yup." He laughed. "Is it working?"

Parker drew a breath. "Actually, yeah. I never wanted to go backward. Always forward."

"You can still do that. You don't have to be physically moving from one place to another to be moving yourself forward." He let Parker chew on that.

He was getting to the bottom of the list, and almost out of advice. He wasn't sure how much more he could stretch stuff.

"Okay, let's say I give it a year. I get my GED, my license, save up some money. Are you and Caleb going to let me stay until I get there?"

"Until you're secure enough to either find a place or you find your next road. I'm not going to do what your father did. Again, there would be rules."

Parker sighed in a classic exaggerated style. "What rules?"

"Our bedroom is always off limits. It's just courtesy. We would do the same for your room. You pay rent for it; it becomes your private space. No illegal shit. As Terra said once, you now live with a cop. Jasper's not a big city, and we both know that, but use your head and stay out of trouble."

"Anything else?"

Ian thought for a few seconds. "Never be scared to ask. One of us will always be able to talk to you. We won't sugarcoat shit, either. Pull your share around the house. We all work, so there's no princess syndrome going on."

"Prince," he half-assed breathed.

Ian rolled his eyes. "No prince crap, either. Roommates would be more appropriate. We're not your father, and neither one of us want to be."

"Equal?"

"As much as can be."

Parker had fallen silent as Ian grabbed the last items on the list. They went through the checkout lane, and Parker helped load the groceries into the bed of the truck. Ian clipped the seatbelt into place and cranked the motor to get the AC blasting like February into the cab.

Parker turned to him and held out his hand. "A year. I'll stay at the shop, get my GED and my license."

"Fair enough. When we get home, we'll figure out a fair cost for the room that won't take your whole check." He shook.

They left the parking lot and Ian scratched his chin. "I'm glad you decided to stay."

Parker twisted on the seat. "Why?" Parker was one of those people that once he let you in, he didn't hide anything. It was clear he hadn't been expecting Ian to say that by his wide eyes.

"Because I'd have to hunt you down to get Summer to stop crying. You've never heard anything like that girl's lungs in full meltdown."

"Can't have that," Parker agreed, amused.

* * * *

The remainder of the evening, Ian spent boxing up what Terra had left behind to put in the attic. She'd moved to Texas to be with Aaron the previous summer and hadn't looked back. Her big, pink, carnival mascot was one of those treasures that had to remain. He needed his own zip code in a room.

"You can leave the dog. He's good company."

Ian tugged on a pink ear. "You sure?" Ian gave him a questioning head tip. "He's obviously a talkative SOB."

Parker chucked one of Terra's smaller lap pillows at his head. It was decided then. Pink was staying.

A lot of drawers were already empty. Parker started dividing his belongings among them. It only took a minute or two. He didn't have much.

Ian hid the heartache as he continued to toss small, loose knickknacks into a box. How could he have gone for so long with so little? Knowing he could have just as easily died out there on any given night and Parker's father not only wouldn't have known, Ian doubted he'd really have cared, solidified his need to do something to help the boy get his feet under him again.

He remembered how hard it had been on both him and Terra when Maria, his sister and Terra's mother, had died. He supposed in some regards, that was what had happened to Parker. Everything he'd once known was now dead to him.

Books, CDs that she hadn't taken, mementos from school, he wouldn't get rid of any of it, but if Parker was going to be in the room, he supposed something a little less girly all around would make him more comfortable.

"Sorry about the mirror." Ian shook his head when he noticed it. *How many hot actors could one girl moon over?*

"Why? Eye candy is eye candy."

He stood with a box in his hands. "I completely forgot." His brow furrowed. "We might need to hash out company rules."

Parker sat on the bed with a bounce, as though enjoying it now that he'd be in it regularly. "Why? It's not like I'm cruising bars."

Ian sat with him. "Yeah, I know. We're getting to know you, and we're fine with that, and you. I just don't know how I'd feel having another someone in the house." *Damn, this just got complicated.* This was one thing he hadn't even considered. When Terra was there and Aaron had stayed over, he'd slept in the spare. Unfortunately, the spare wasn't equipped for guests any longer.

"Don't worry about it. I'm beginning to see a good thing happening here. I'm not going to fuck it up by bringing home a one-night stand."

And that was one of those small reminders that for his age, Parker may have more common sense than the average twenty year-old.

He stood from the bed. "Okay, I'm taking this one up, then starting dinner. If you find anything else that you want taken up, just box it or let me know."

Parker bunched up the comforter. "I think the first thing I'm going to do is buy sheets that aren't this light purple."

"Don't blame you." Ian smiled as he left the room.

And that was that. Parker was officially living with them.

Chapter Nine

Will turned off Main Street to the highway late Saturday morning. The fairgrounds were about two miles out of town, the Sheriff's Posse Arena, a new addition to the county from what Tammie had told him. He hadn't been to a carnival in years. He hadn't been out much since coming to Jasper in March and after six months, figured he should know a little more than he did. That he should know more people than just the patients he saw at the dentist office. He didn't want to be the continual stranger, Dr. Parkinson—who's filling in for Dr. Kirkpatrick—forever.

He didn't believe in religion, though he understood the spirituality of it, so he had no desire to attend one of the many churches in town. His mother had very strong faith ideas, but none of them were founded in a religion. Mostly it was doing good for others, sharing when a man could, and even when he couldn't. There had been many times the only reason they had food some nights was for the good grace of another's generosity. And there was always someone within reach who needed what you could give them, be it a word of support, a hot meal, or like Ian had done for Parker, stability to start over.

Will hadn't known about Ian at all two weeks ago, but he'd gotten an earful since Parker's first visit for his tooth. He'd never put much stock in rumors or opinions, but there had to be some foundation to them. He was willing to bet the man was as good as

Tammie had made him out to be. And then he'd also gotten another list for his husband, Caleb. Both good, upstanding men in the community.

Not long after making his turn, he spotted a person walking along the highway. He wore a beat up, gray cowboy hat, and had tucked a longer shirt into his back waist, wearing just an A-shirt in the summer heat.

He realized he knew who this was the closer he got. He passed him and pulled to the side of road, rolling to a slow stop while watching him in the rearview mirror. Will had time to stretch across the seats and open the door for Parker before he reached the car.

"Hey, Dr. Parkinson. Thanks." He gave a broad smile, swinging the door shut.

"It's Will, if I never mentioned. Why are you walking?" He waited for Parker to buckle up before putting the car in gear.

"Faster than crawling," he answered evenly. Then his playful smile lit his face. "Ian's at the shop for a few more hours and Caleb's asleep. I told them I'd find a way to get out to the fairgrounds."

"It's got to be a hundred and eight, and you're walking in it."

"It's ninety-three, or was when I left the house, and it's only two miles. I used to cover twenty in a day." He pulled his shirt forward and laid it over his lap. "Thanks for stopping."

"You're welcome."

"Where are you from? I can't really tell with your voice." He held up a hand. "Not that I don't like it, but even a deaf dog can tell with me."

Will harrumphed once in humor. "Florida. Daytona area originally."

"Wow. And you left the beach and bikinis for *this*?" Youthful flabbergasted teasing.

Will didn't correct him. If Parker thought he was straight, or straight enough, then he could deal with having him in the car. His sun warmed skin was tanned, and begging for touch, and even the distance between them didn't diminish the scent of the sunshine on his body.

"I know. I need my head examined." He slowed the car as they approached the grounds, joining the caravan of vehicles getting directed to park. "Okay, I'll tell you a secret, but you can't breathe a word until it's public. Deal?" He guessed they had a few minutes as vehicles of all sorts crept into place.

"Sure." Parker raised his hat to give him a straight stare.

"John Kirkpatrick isn't on leave, or vacation. He's taking reduced hours to let me slide into the practice. He's retiring in a few more months."

"Seriously?"

"It's an established practice but because of the location, there weren't many takers to come talk to him about buying him out. I think there was me and two others who were supposed to interview with him. He didn't want to completely close and leave the town without any care. So he came up with this. A changing of the guard kind of move."

"How'd you get the practice?"

"By default, I guess. One didn't come to the state at all, and the other interviewed but apparently, John didn't care for her." He'd never repeat it, but he'd actually said she was a sanctimonious twat and he'd never leave his practice in hands like hers.

"Well, I have a knowledgeable dislike of dentists. You belong here."

"Thank you," he said, pleased at the compliment. "I try to make it as pleasant as possible. No one likes to be there to begin with. Why make it that much harder to just get through?"

"True."

"How long are you staying today?" Will got out of the car, waiting for him at the front.

"Until after the rodeo this afternoon. I want to see the bull riders."

"I'm looking forward to that too. I'm a team roper fan myself."

"Really? You like rodeo?" His excitement ramped up again.

"The finesse and timing kill me." Hard chests, rock solid thighs. What wasn't to love?

He slid a hand into a front pocket. It was too hot for him for jeans like Parker wore. Light pants and walking shoes. He'd never owned a pair of cowboy boots in his life.

"Vandersoot is your last name, right?"

Will had never killed anyone's excitement so quickly in his life by mentioning their last name.

"Yeah." Parker looked away. It might have been a hundred degrees under the sun, but it had to have dropped fifty degrees in seconds, the fun chilled so fast between them. "Let me guess. You're a Chet fan, too."

"For his skill. I've heard his audios. He's an ass."

Parker sneered in complete disgust. "You know that's my father, right?"

"Do you want me to apologize?" Will slowed to study the younger man. Had he been reading the situation wrong?

"I just wish you didn't worship him too," he muttered. He took a step away and jammed his hat down on his head. "Thanks for the ride. I'll see you around."

He spun on a heel in the dried and packed grass and actually made it a few feet before Will realized what he'd done.

"Parker! Wait."

Catching up and looking into his face, Parker had completely shut down. All the sparkle of a shared pastime was missing from his gaze.

"I don't worship the man. I just told you he was an ass, but I can respect his skill."

"He's the one who busted my tooth." Anger made Parker's eyes glitter in the sunlight. "He disowned me, threatened to have me arrested and thrown in jail. Threatened to have my best friend arrested. He even said he'd go and see it done."

"Why?" Will was struck numb by the anger and hatred one man could show his own son.

"For kissing my best friend."

Will hissed.

"Want to know how I know how long it's been?" he asked, anger vibrating his voice with a deathly calm. Every word was a snarl through a tight jaw growing white under the pressure.

Will wasn't sure he did.

"Three days before my birthday was the day my entire life ended. Over a fucking kiss. So I'm sorry I can't share your respect or admiration." He took a step away and touched the brim of his hat. "I hope you enjoy the rodeo. Thanks again for the ride."

This time, when he spun and stomped into the distance, Will didn't try to stop him.

* * * *

Parker put his shirt on, but left it open, hanging loose. Without knowing the arena, it took time to find the staging area for the riders, which was fine. It gave him time to cool down after losing it with Will.

He wasn't mad *at* Will. He just hadn't expected to feel so let down hearing that Will admired his dad so much.

"Anyone know Travis Hopeck?"

A guy hanging on a gate tossed a thumb over his shoulder. "Saw him this morning over by the trailer yard."

"Thanks!" He turned and jogged away from the pens, hunting for the RVs and horse trailers.

He spotted a truck that looked like it could be Travis' and hesitantly studied it. He didn't recognize the trailer. It was newer than the one he used to haul. But that was four years ago. He walked around the other side.

And smiled as elation wiped away the earlier episode with Will.

He walked up to the sorrel horse munching on hay and started to pet its face. "Hey, Snowman. How you been?"

Parker's eyes hurt from building pressure as he petted the horse's flat face. He missed Chaser so much. He hadn't thought about him much in the last couple of years. He'd longed for his horse daily when he'd been sitting under bridges and scared out of his mind that he was going to die. They'd had the ranch dogs, but Chaser was his hoofed friend. The one who never argued and always listened.

He blinked, feeling the tracks on his cheeks before he could control them. So many things taken from him. His entire life. Gone.

"Parker?"

He quickly scrubbed a palm over his cheeks then turned to face Travis. He held his riding number in a hand.

Parker didn't know whether to jump him or shake hands.

Travis took the initiative, grasping him by his shirt collar and engulfing him in muscled arms. Shock made him stiff for a heartbeat, then he went limp, hanging on like he was drowning and Travis was a log in a river.

He held on for what felt like days. He didn't remark when he felt one of them tremble. Parker didn't even know which of them did it.

Eventually, Parker leaned to be able to take in all of Travis. He looked so much like the boy he'd cared for, the one he'd palled around with for most of his life. But he was older now, too. He'd filled out and he swore... He was looking up at the bastard now. "You grew," he remarked, clearing his throat when the words got caught.

"You did, too." He shook Parker by the shoulders. "Damn, it's good to see you."

Parker released him, one hand rising to Travis' jaw. A mishmash of scars marked his neck and his lower jaw on one side. He cupped the reminders of pain that Parker hadn't been there to help him through. "He did a number on you, didn't he?" It was easy to see how his voice box had been damaged. It was a miracle Travis hadn't lost his head by the tale of those scars alone.

"Fucker tried to kill me. Was in a damn jaw trap for four months."

"They wired you?"

"Lost almost thirty pounds because of it."

"You found them again," Parker retorted, poking at his tight gut. "I'm sorry about your dad." He knew it needed to be said.

"It's okay. The fight was bad, but it was my accident on top of it that was too much for him. I've been holding my own." He looked over his shoulder. "There's someone I want you to meet."

"Oh?" Parker let his hand fall free. That was when he noticed the second halter and rope tied to the side of the trailer. Whatever thin and fragile hopes he'd started to spin with reconnecting with his best friend from his old life, splintered to the ground like frozen spider webs.

"Eddie Flores. He's around here somewhere." He looked over his shoulder then back. Sadness darkened his gaze. "By the way, your dad sold Chaser. I tried to get him, but he refused to sell him to me."

"Fuck!" Parker slumped against the trailer wall. "Did he go to a good buyer, at least?"

"I really don't know. For what he was asking, someone had to want him bad. I'm sorry."

"No, it's okay. Nothing you could do about it." He let out a breath, hoping Chaser had found a good home. "Did he give you any shit?" They both knew what Parker was asking.

"No. He kept quiet. Never brought it up, or talked to Dad. I think people went by his house asking about you and where you were."

"Probably told them I'd run off," he muttered, kicking at dried earth. His dad sure wouldn't take any of that blame. That was one person he knew he'd never want to talk to again.

"When did your dad find out?" Parker started buttoning his shirt to tuck it in.

"About a year and a half ago. He caught me kissing Eddie good luck. So, I told him the truth." He rolled a shoulder.

Parker groaned. "Oh, fuck. Serious?"

Travis sighed. "Yeah." So they'd been together a while. He wasn't going to mess that up for his friend. What he said next confirmed it. "This is my first full season back since I jacked up my throat." Eddie had been with him through the worst. That was a good mark for Travis' boyfriend right there. What that meant was it hadn't been all that long ago since Travis' life was also turned on its ear. Parker was glad to see him doing so well and happy.

"Well, I came to watch you ride." He resettled his hat on his head, shaking off the memories and wishful clinging thoughts.

Travis reached forward and played with Parker's longer hair. "This looks good."

"*Bonito*, you better not be flirtin' with that good lookin' cowboy."

Parker searched beyond Travis and spotted a cowboy sitting on a solid palomino. Laughter lightened his expression under his hat, his whole face radiating the affection he felt for Travis when he looked at him. He may have been teasing, but his entire focus was Travis.

Yeah, definitely a good man for his friend.

Travis twisted to search over his shoulder and laughed. "Told you he was hot."

Parker's face flushed with embarrassment.

Eddie chuckled as he slid from his saddle, leading his horse up. He stuck out a hand. "*Con mucho gusto*. Travis has told me a lot about you."

"Nice to meet you, too. I hope it was mostly good things," he replied.

"Eh, bad things build character, nice things build reputation. You need both."

Parker arched an eyebrow, and Travis rolled his eyes. "He loves reading philosophical non-fiction when we're driving places."

Eddie tied up his horse. "It passes the time." He stroked the horse's neck, making sure he was comfortable, loosening its saddle girth as a last thing. "Draco is warmed up. Let's go get something to drink."

Chapter Ten

The three strolled toward the open arena. "So, spill. Where have you been?"

Parker walked with Travis between him and Eddie. "Stayed in Texas for about a year. Houston, then Dallas. Managed to get a little money here and there, went to Louisiana and Arkansas. Bummed around until I started going west, and landed in Jasper by dumb luck." He didn't go into detail. Some things were better left in the past.

"You're living here?" Travis asked at his shoulder.

"For the next year. I lucked into being found by a couple of really good men." Parker explained the deal, the job, and his plans. "After that year, I'll see what I want to do. If there's more school, or something like that."

"So, what? They adopted you?" Eddie shook his head in disbelief. "Aren't many like that on this planet."

"No, there aren't." Parker adjusted his hat for the sun. "But yeah, I guess they did. And once that happened, the whole family took me in. They're loud and insane." *And awesome.*

"Jasper doesn't seem big enough for it," Travis mused.

"I think it's Ian and Caleb who have done the most to wake this sleepy hole up."

"You admire them," Travis remarked.

"Incredibly." No doubt about it.

"There's one of the soda pop stands. You want one, *Bonito*?"

"I'd love something. Parker?"

"You buy, and I'll get the next round." Thankfully, he had cash from his first check in his wallet.

Eddie smiled. "Deal."

They were standing in line when Parker heard the high-pitched cry of his name. Turning, he spotted Summer coming at him at a full-tilt run.

He lowered to a knee and caught her, the impact sending both to the ground in a heap of laughter.

"Summer Denise!"

"Uh oh," she whispered, her blue eyes going saucer wide as her laughter dried up with a squeak.

"It's okay." He sat up, dusting her off to put her on her feet, then did the same for himself. Once he'd managed to clean most of his butt and hers, he straightened his hat then bent and scooped her up.

"Summer, you apologize to Parker right now, young lady." Wanda was *not* happy, scowling as only a mother could.

"I'm sorry," she said, then dove into his neck to hide.

"Don't cry, baby girl," he said, sweeping her back. She was a trembling body of bones, fearing her mother's wrath.

"She said she saw you, not that she was going to audition as a linebacker."

"She'd be good," Travis said, snickering to hide the worst of it. "You were just taken down by forty-five pounds of pure fluff."

"Bite me," Parker retorted. "Wanda, these are friends of mine. Travis and Eddie. And this powerhouse is Summer."

She raised her head and wiped her eyes. "He's my big brother."

Parker caught Travis' expression, one highly arched eyebrow. "A brother now, huh?"

"Have you seen anyone else? We just got here," Wanda asked.

"No, I haven't been here that long. Ian and Caleb said they'd be around after Ian closes the shop."

"Mama, can I stay with Parker for a little while?"

Wanda was about to say no, but he cut her off. "If it's okay with you, I can show her some of the animals." They were going in that direction anyway.

She studied him for a few seconds. "You'll keep an eye on her? You just saw how fast she can move."

Parker looked Summer straight in the eye. "Will you listen? If you don't, I'll never do anything like this again."

She gulped. "Never?"

"Never."

She clung tighter. "I'll listen."

"Damn. If Jeannie could see this," she muttered. "Okay. Do you have a phone?"

When Parker started to shake his head, Travis came to the rescue. "I do."

They did a number swap.

"I want to see what's keeping Jeannie. I'll call in a bit and see if you're exhausted or not." She gave a few last dire warnings to Summer and then with a final pecked kiss for her daughter, left Parker to watch Summer.

* * * *

Will walked around the large bull pens. The big beasts looked drowsy in the heat. He had his doubts that they would stay that way. He was trying to be mindful of where he stepped. The stench was powerful in the hot sun, exacerbating things he didn't want to examine too closely along with the hay, water, dust, and sweat. How anyone could be around cattle all day, every day, confounded him. He'd seen the calves and they even had a pen for sheep. Mutton busting. He'd seen it before and it always made him question the survival of the human species. It did make him smile, picturing kids clinging like little monkeys to the back of a sheep. Brave kids. Or foolish. At least they wore safety gear.

"Parker, can I pet the cows?"

"No, baby girl. Those are bulls, and they aren't nice to little girls. They eat little girls like you."

Will raised his head, and his gaze landed right on the man. He was squatted down, grasping one of the metal fence barriers around the inner holding pen, talking to a young girl and holding one of her hands. His jeans curved like a wet dream to his shape; he knew what Parker looked like under his shirt. Unfortunately, he could recall those details almost too well from that morning. Not what he wanted to fixate on.

Parker must have sensed someone watching him because he happened to pick that moment to glance up, and their gazes locked.

Will didn't know if he should turn away or not. Parker had been fully irate with him not that long ago.

Parker stood without losing Will's gaze. The young girl didn't seem aware that they'd started walking in his direction.

"Hey," Parker said quietly. He glanced down and smiled for her. "Summer, this is Will. He's a friend, too."

She looked up but seemed utterly sucked in by the large bulls behind the rails.

"Am I a friend?" Will asked.

Parker faced him. "Yeah. Sorry about this morning. I shouldn't have gone off the handle like that. You didn't do anything wrong."

"I can understand how it hurt you though," Will told him. "I wasn't trying to."

"I know." He gazed down at the young girl, then looking at Will through his lashes asked, "Want to hang out with us?"

Should say no. But he couldn't. "Sure."

"Travis and Eddie are on the other side talking to some rep guy. I told them we'd see the pens then I'd meet up with them again."

Will fell into step with them, dawdling appropriately so Summer could see the animals. He had a thousand questions. Who were Travis and Eddie? Why was Summer with Parker?

Why couldn't he stop thinking about the younger man? He knew now, without a doubt, that Parker was gay. Will also knew that was the path to trouble.

The three of them walked down an alley created by the walls of guard fencing. Will couldn't help himself. He took a deep breath of fresher air when they reached the end.

Parker lowly laughed at him. "It takes getting used to."

"I'll take your word for it. I swear my nose will never be the same."

"City boy," Parker teased. "There's Travis."

They joined the other two, and Parker made introductions. They walked for a while longer, then Travis and Eddie said they had to get their gear ready for their rounds.

"Good luck guys." Parker faced Travis. "Ride safe."

"Always." Travis gave him a poignant smile then sauntered away, Eddie at his side.

"So he was the one, wasn't he?" Will hadn't missed the underlying current between them.

"He was. He's still my friend, but he's doing well with Eddie now."

They walked into a thicker milling crowd as people began arriving for the rodeo. Parker stopped short and cursed under his breath. "Oh, crap. I just remembered. Travis had Wanda's phone number. I'll have to watch for her."

"Summer's mom?"

"Yeah." He jiggled the young girl's hand. "We're okay, though. Right, baby girl?"

She nodded, skipping over tufts of grass.

"Who is she?"

"Friend's daughter. Summer wanted to see the livestock, and it didn't look like Wanda really wanted to." He leaned close. "I think Wanda took advantage of the fact that she seems to want to listen to me." He grinned impishly. "I don't mind. She's a good kid." He stopped them both and asked, "Baby girl, did your Mama or Mimi say if anyone else was coming to the rodeo?"

"Jus' Mama and Mimi."

"Okay. Ian and Caleb are coming but I don't know when."

"Parker, I'm getting hungry," she said.

"Well, let's see what there is for young cowgirls like you."

She smiled happily, going back to her skipping.

"You are good with her. Did you have brothers or sisters?"

"No. I was an only child. Mom divorced Dad when I was seven. Can't say I blame her, looking back now. Dad was—" His gaze flicked south to Summer. "Well, he caused that tooth. I'll leave it at that."

Will nodded.

"I was mad at her for years, but not now. She probably would have died," he added quietly to keep Summer from overhearing. "Travis was like a brother and my best friend all in one."

"I guess it's good luck you found him here, then."

"Good luck or dumb luck." He snorted. "Just luck. Not laughing at fate anymore. It's been good since Grint picked me up."

"Oh?"

Parker regaled him with the story of his first day and night in Jasper, with Ian and Caleb.

"So, how long will you be staying?" Will had assumed since the beginning it wouldn't be for long. Parker's answer took him by surprise.

"I promised Ian a year. I'll be twenty-one in another week." He patted Summer's hair. "I want to make a change, and I think it's now or never."

Will swallowed thickly, hearing the determination and emotion in Parker's words. He might have been younger than Parker when it all hit the fan, but he remembered all too well those moments, and the feelings that went with them.

"Crazy hot today." Parker scratched under his hat then replaced it. Will wanted to dump that hat and run his fingers through Parker's golden brown hair. He kept his hands at his sides, listening instead, with probably far too much interest.

Everything he was hearing said Parker was a levelheaded young man. He had a good heart, could handle children and animals, and as he rediscovered himself, apparently knew with more and more confidence what he was going to do with life.

All the more to like and admire.

Which of course meant he was driving Will slowly out of his mind, grinding down all his reasons to avoid getting to know the younger man better.

"Hey, there's a hotdog stand." Will pointed toward it, glad to finally have a diversion.

"What do you say, Summer?"

"Hotdog! Hotdog!" She started leapfrogging in that direction.

"I think you picked a winner."

The smile Parker gave him almost melted him into his shoes. He tried to blame the bright sunlight and heat, but inside, he knew the truth.

Chapter Eleven

Parker carried all the hotdogs slathered in ketchup, relish, and mustard for Will, who had offered to help carry the drinks. Summer was doing her share too, carrying a handful of napkins for everyone. It had been a long time since he'd bought concession food. He hoped he'd been able to hide his shock at the cost.

"Let's go to the arena and just find a spot. The preshow will be starting soon anyway."

Will nodded in answer and Parker led them up the bleachers.

"Remember what your mama said, Summer. Listen, because it's going to get really noisy and crowded here soon."

"I promise."

"That's my baby sis, huh?" He leaned down to give her a smile and got a shock. She kissed him on the cheek.

"I don't know who has who wrapped around which finger more, but you two are a pair." Will's rumbled laughter made him smile.

Parker wasn't going to argue. He knew Summer was being on her best behavior.

"This is good." Parker sat. They were a few rows up and on the end of the arena with the chutes. A clear view of Travis and Eddie was all he was asking for. That and safe rides for both.

With Summer sitting between the two men in anticipation of the rodeo, they chowed down on the hotdogs until they were gone. Parker answered questions, keeping Summer entertained until the parade horses and 4-H clubs started their intros. Honestly, it was probably better that Summer wanted to be distracted and that she was between them. He was liking the time spent with Will.

Parker had caught him smiling a whole lot more than before, and he was right. He had a dimple on the right side. Just as innocent as you please, and then he'd smile and Parker couldn't help but think how good it looked. The dimple and those smiles.

"It looks like they're going to start with calf roping." Parker pointed to the opposite end where men were milling about.

"Does it hurt the baby cows?"

Parker smiled, sharing it with Will. "Nope. In fact, this is a technique that's been used by cowboys for hundreds of years to ground a calf. They just added timers and belt buckles as prizes for the fastest. Watch the cowboy's hands when he gets down to the calf. Bet you won't see them move 'til he's done."

"Nuh uh!" she argued in disbelief.

He crossed his arms and stretched his shoulders to lean backward a little, hamming it up for her. "Are you doubtin' a real life cowboy, sayin' he's lyin'?" He rolled his accent deep, making her laugh. "Watch. There are some very fast guys who do this."

She gasped when the first contender roped the calf, slid off his horse at a run, knelt and tossed his hands in seconds.

She cheered with everyone else, bouncing up and down on her bottom. "I didn't see anything!"

Parker leaned close. "Told ya," he said.

The calf roping went into the team roping and the steer wrestling. Summer was completely enthralled in the whole process.

Will spoke over her head. "I think you've created a lifelong fan."

Parker turned to answer, grinning at her shared enthusiasm and the energy of the rodeo itself. And snagged on gray eyes. Will's face was flushed from the heat and the excitement.

He was smiling. The full smile with the dimple. The one he just learned could make his toes curl.

Parker's mouth went dry. He tried to swallow, and couldn't. The eyes watching him darkened a notch. Heavy lashes lowered a fraction.

Parker's heart beat into his chest so hard, he felt its echo.

God, I want to kiss him. Want to kiss him so badly.

A cheer erupted around them, jerking them apart. Parker gasped a breath or two, trying to catch up to what was going on. He felt lightheaded.

Watching two riders make a victory lap around the arena, he figured it out. The top scorers for the roping events had been called.

Feeling a little more in control after a moment, he shifted to glance sideways and found Will watching the arena. Nowhere else. Definitely not looking toward Parker. Disappointment knifed through him.

He guessed that kiss he was thinking about was all him, and all wishful thinking. It didn't seem Will really had any interest in Parker like that.

That had been miles stronger than what he remembered happening in the dental office. Same kind of urgency. Same kind of...*something*. Desire?

Was he feeling honest desire for the quiet man? It was something to think about. He hadn't felt want or attraction for another person like this, not since those initial youthful urges with Travis. He'd had sex, and usually that had felt nice, but it was unattached and had been a means to an end.

This didn't feel anything like that. At all. He was kind of glad of that fact.

A kiss would only be the beginning, if he got the chance, and it would probably be the ultimate end for any kind of friendship between them.

Will hadn't given one vibe that he was interested in Parker. Unsure of what to do, or how to approach Will, especially if he did get the chance for a kiss, he pushed it away for the moment.

He couldn't and wouldn't do anything while he was caring for Summer. Because the kind of kiss he really wanted would be raunchy at its heart. Not exactly conducive to attempt in front of an audience, the child beside him, or the thousand or so surrounding him.

"Now what are they doing?"

Parker focused to the arena, glad for the interruption out of his thoughts. They were setting up the barrel racing triangle, raking out the soft ground for steadier footing for the animals. "They're going to do the barrels. This is a lady's event. Fast horses and light hands."

Summer cheered. "Yay! Girl power!"

Parker snickered, and he realized Will did too. "That is all her mothers' doing."

"I don't doubt it," Will remarked, flashing gray eyes and another one of those sexy smiles at him.

Good Lord, get to the bulls. Please. He faced forward, Summer following the horses as they flew through the rounds and thundered past them for the gate timer.

Summer tugged on his shirt sleeve during the next lull. "There's the bulls!" She pointed, her whole body vibrating.

Parker looked toward the chutes and spotted the lumbering animals being herded into place. They prepped the animals one chute at a time, distracting the crowds with the antics of children clinging to sheep. Parker caught Will's chuckled smirks as, one by one, the kids went down. They were hardy little things, being jostled and tossed. The kid with the longest time got a trophy and a picture with the rodeo queen.

He remembered watching those scenes play out dozens of times when he was younger, working and training his way up to ride bulls. There was a certain fondness for those days, a nostalgia that he hadn't realized he'd feel, watching as a spectator, not a contestant.

The arena cleared, and they brought out the clowns. *Time to get real.*

The announcer started giving the stats for the first rider as he straddled the bull and tightened the strap, the resonating sound of the bell ringing as the animal twitched beneath the rider. The animal whipped out of the chute like a tornado on hooves. Summer's little hand gripped onto his until the rider had been thrown off and ran for the arena wall to avoid the irate animal.

"Give that young man a round of applause," the announcer said, giving his numbers.

"Is that a good score?" Will asked.

"It's fair, beatable, but he rode well. It's half the rider, half the bull. You draw a dud and it doesn't matter if you're tap dancing on his back, you'll tank."

"Does that happen often?"

Will watched the next rider prep for takeoff. "The bulls are picked because they can move, but like a person, they have off days."

The next chute rolled open, and the poor guy didn't last two seconds, being jackknifed into the bull's jumps.

"Ouch," Parker said in commiseration.

The rider grabbed his hat off the ground and scooted for the opposite side gates as the rodeo clowns did their gig and herded the bull toward the exit alley.

"Next up in chute number three, Travis Hopeck."

Parker's tension rose. Summer leaned into him. He held his breath until he saw Travis give the okay and then held it for eight seconds more.

The coppery red beast exploded out of the gate with a flying jump, bucking and tossing its weight around. Parker swore he felt the reverberations as it landed on front hooves, the shockwave shooting an intense ripple of energy across skin and muscle. Clouds of dust burst upward beneath each landing. Saliva flew in thick, gnarly ropes from the beast as it grunted and did its worst, swinging its head as it knifed its body in opposing directions. Travis heeled the bull, spurring around the wide barrel at the right moments, his balance arm high over his head. Parker could tell his skills had really improved over the years. He was stronger, now, fluid. He was riding the bull like a pro.

The snapped actions whipped Travis like a rag doll on his back, but he held on until the buzzer.

"He did it!" Summer cried, cheering for him as he bolted for the side wall when his bull decided to take umbrage at having to work to get rid of that pesky rider.

"Wow," Will choked. "He is really good. That is going to be hard to beat."

Travis managed to take a two point lead over the top score. The applause and cheering rose in appreciation.

There was a rider Parker didn't know, then Eddie finished the lineup. He scored third behind the first rider, but missed being in the money by only two one-hundredths of a point.

"That is a fine shaved hair when it comes to score."

"Fractions," Parker agreed.

Saddle and bronc busting finished up the day. A final cheer was given for all the participants as they rode around the arena at a parade lope, waving hats and hands to all who'd come to watch them.

Parker saw Will check the time on his phone. "Really? Almost two hours?"

"You never notice with all the events and intermissions."

Will tipped Summer up. "We should get her out of the sun. She's going to be a tomato come morning."

Parker peeked at her smiling, little face. *Crap.* Again. "I hope Wanda and Jeannie don't kill me." He searched faces but knew it was hopeless. He wondered if she'd called Travis at all. He was sure she had. Parker doubted Wanda had expected Summer to stay with him all afternoon.

"Where should we start?" Will gazed in both directions.

"Let's get down on the ground. I have an idea."

Parker led them all to a not too busy spot, and lowered to his haunches. "Can you sit on my shoulders and look for your Mama or Uncle Ian?"

She nodded with huge eyes.

"Could you hold this for me?" He handed his hat to Will. "Okay, little lady. One, two, three." He braced her and swung her up over his shoulders, standing straight until both were steady. "Give me your hands." He held her fingers, while she hooked her short legs around his back. "First one to see her gets ice cream." He figured that should keep her looking.

"You're tall!" she cried, a little wobbly and clingy.

He grimaced. "Hardly, but hopefully tall enough."

"You're tall enough for me," Will said at his shoulder.

Parker managed to turn a little to his side, catching the slightest rise of red on the man's neck. Parker wasn't sure he'd heard him right, if he'd even spoken. That could be too much sun that he was mistaking for something else.

"Shouldn't we start looking?"

Parker released a breath as he put a foot forward. He really needed to quit imagining things when it came to Will.

Chapter Twelve

"Can I wear your hat, Parker?"

"Sure, baby girl."

Will handed it up to her and she carefully put it on, giving Parker back her hands when she was satisfied.

"Cowgirl in training," Will said.

"I wanna be a cowgirl and ride bulls!" she exclaimed.

"Uh..." Parker's expression was a cross between lost and terrified. "I've created a menace."

"I see Uncle Ian!" She bounced on his shoulders.

"Where? Does he see you?"

"I think so." She raised her hand and twitched. "He saw." She grasped him again.

"Is he mad? Can you see him, Will?"

"Ah, there he is. He doesn't look upset, but he's on the phone."

"God, they're going to kill me." Parker sounded very nervous, chewing on his lip as they moved forward through the crowd.

Will put a hand on Parker's lower back. "It's fine. All you did was watch the rodeo."

When he realized where his hand was, he pulled it away, hoping Parker hadn't realized what he'd done. It was bad enough what he'd let slip. Hopefully Parker hadn't caught it.

"Let me explain—" Parker said as soon as they were close enough.

"We saw the bulls!" Summer exclaimed with no distinction of voice volume. "Parker let me wear his hat. I want to ride. Can I ride bulls, Uncle Ian?"

Ian came to a stop in front of them, gazing up, looking just as lost and confused as Parker.

"Bulls?" He huffed, his hands rising to his hips. "Okay, honey. One thing at a time. You're fine, Parker."

"I—I am?"

"You wouldn't let anything happen to your baby sister, would you?" he asked with a gentle seriousness that even struck Will's nerves. She wasn't Will's sister, and he knew he'd fight dragons for her. He also realized what Ian was trying to convey by giving Parker that title. He was family, and trusted with Summer. It looked like the good rumors about Ian were more than true. If anything, they were lacking in the light of reality.

"Never," Parker croaked.

"Come here, girl. Give Parker's shoulders a break." He reached for her, and Parker stooped to let her be plucked over his head. He teetered with the loss of weight, and Will slid a few inches behind a shoulder to steady him, his hand on Parker's waist.

It was closer than he thought, and apparently unexpected because Parker sank into his chest for a heartbeat.

"Oh, sorry," Parker whispered, averting his gaze when he stood straight.

"You're fine." Will wished he hadn't been so fast to stand.

"So, where were you heading?" Ian asked.

"Looking for Wanda or Jeannie," Parker explained. "Wanted to find Travis to congratulate him on his win."

"I think the girls want to get this one home before it gets too much later."

"No!"

Everyone jerked to a freezing stop.

"I want to stay with Parker!"

"Honey, your Mama and Mimi are waiting for you." Ian tried to placate her, but it was obviously not what she wanted to hear.

"But..." Her lip started to tremble, proof she was getting tired.

"Baby girl, I'm not going anywhere. I'll be there for breakfast tomorrow."

"Promise?" She flashed blue eyes at him that would crack a less determined person.

God, she can turn the screws on a man. Will watched all of this with a lot of fascination and a little fear. What would she be like as a teenager?

"I promise."

"You better give him back his hat," Ian instructed. "A cowboy isn't a cowboy without his hat."

She handed it over.

"If you need a ride home, we'll be here for a little while," Ian said.

Parker shrugged. "If nothing else, I can get Travis to take me."

"Or me," Will said quietly, not wanting to intrude if he wasn't wanted.

Parker swiveled on his neck and blinked. "Or Will," he repeated for Ian. "You guys have fun. I won't be late." He scooted close and gave Summer a kiss on the cheek. "Love you, baby girl."

"You too, Parker." She smooched him back.

"She has you so wrapped around her finger," Will commented with a slight snicker as they watched the pair walk away.

Parker resettled his hat, hiding his blushing cheeks if Will had to guess. "Come on. I need to go give Travis some hell or his head's going to get big over that win."

* * * *

The sun set on the world, and the carnival lit it right back up. Parker rubbed his stomach. He was getting hungry, his stomach rumbling. The downfall of getting used to eating. You got *used to eating*. He sighed. He wasn't about to pay for concession food again, though.

Someone's stomach made a loud noise. He was about to make an excuse that it was probably him when Will asked, "Hey, do you think Lucy's is still open?"

"I really don't know." Though Parker half hoped she would be. He could afford a hot plate at least.

Will nudged him with an elbow. "Let's go see. I'm starving. Hotdogs only go so far."

Parker agreed, trying to downplay his enthusiasm. They spent a little longer than he'd originally expected with Travis and Eddie, talking and hanging out. It still took him by surprise to catch them holding hands, or even once, kissing. Ian and Caleb he was growing accustomed to, but seeing others do the same thing still made him freeze up. It wasn't even intentional. It just happened.

"Do you want to call Ian and let him know?" Will offered on their way to the parking lot.

"Probably should."

Will handed over his phone, and Parker dialed Ian's cell. After a quick few words, he handed it back. "I think that might be the next thing on my list." He really wanted the dentist bill paid first.

Leaving the arena grounds and driving into town took only a few minutes.

"Damn." Will tapped the steering wheel when he pulled into a space on the street in front of the doors. "She just closed. Says nine."

"That's okay. I guess I'll go home, then." Parker could slap lunchmeat on to bread. He wasn't about to try to cook. *That* was a skill he was very out of practice with.

"I can probably make something quick at my place, if you're okay with that." Will half faced him on the seat. "I'll take you home before it's too late, but I'm starving."

"Okay, sure."

Will had that car in reverse and moving before Parker had finished speaking.

"You must be hungry," he joked at the man's impatience.

"You haven't heard the dinosaur between us? I think I'm so hollow, I'm echoing."

Parker groaned in embarrassment. "I thought that was me!"

Will shot him a wide-eyed look, then laughed quietly. He rolled to a stop in the driveway of large, ranch-style home. The porch was wide and went from end to end. A single yellow light illuminated the front. He half expected someone's mother to open the door, ready to scold them for being out after dark.

"Wow, this is a nice place."

"Thanks. I'm renting, but I've been talking to the owner about just buying it outright. I love it. It's homey and natural, and there's a huge barn in the back that he subleases separately for horses and pasture."

"Really?"

"Yeah. One of these days, I'd like to have one or two and learn how to ride. It's been in the back of my mind for a while and one of the reasons why when I found this and it was available, I snapped it up quick." They walked up to the front door together. "The owner told me at one time he had huge urns here filled with flowers that his wife had cared for."

"Where are they?"

Will unlocked the door and opened it for Parker. "When she passed away, he sold them. He said they were her hobby." He closed the door and turned on a light. "Welcome to my home."

Parker could see his instant love for the home. "Wow. This looks like one of those homes you see on the cable networks. Rustic and well-cared for."

"You see it, too." Will smiled and Parker felt himself melting again for that smile. "That's what I fell in love with. A fresh coat of paint outside and a good scrub and polish on the floors inside. I'm really hoping he'll let me buy it from him."

"What's stopping him?"

"It's a city historical site, so he has to get approval, and I have to agree to maintain it to a certain degree to its original form."

"Will you?"

"In a heartbeat. I don't want to change a thing." Parker followed as Will led him from the door to the kitchen. "The heritage site rule only applies to the house. I can change anything outside of a set distance of the structure—a buffer zone, I guess—add behind it, or to the barn."

"How much land does it have?"

"Almost three hundred total acres."

Wow. That was even more than they'd had in Texas.

Will opened the refrigerator and began pulling out vegetables and sliced meat. "This will be quick and filling."

"Quick is the word I care about."

"Totally."

In less than fifteen minutes, he had thick wraps rolled, cut, and on plates. "I rarely do this so late, but chips okay?"

"Sure."

They sat down at the table together, and Parker rested his hat to the side. They both dug in almost in unison.

Will pointed behind Parker's shoulder a moment later. "Reach behind you and grab some drinks from the fridge."

"No soda pop?" he asked when he looked, teasing the other man. Of course a dentist wouldn't have soda.

"My ills lean towards coffee, and the occasional soda."

Parker handed over the water bottle, winking to let Will know he didn't mean anything by it. He barely breathed after that, wolfing down the food in front of him. He wasn't used to being comfortable with what he was eating yet, that it wouldn't be the last thing he saw for days or longer.

They were both starving for dinner, so maybe Will wouldn't notice.

When he glanced up, he just caught Will's dropping gaze, returning to his own food.

"Sorry," he mumbled, feeling like an ass. Will wasn't going to steal his food from him. He needed to find it in himself to try to trust again. Some things, he was discovering, were simply harder than others to accept. He hadn't realized he'd probably been doing this at home, too. Neither Ian nor Caleb had remarked on it. Silently, he knew they wouldn't. They weren't the types to pressure him to be something he wasn't. And right now he'd discovered, he was still gun shy and protective about food.

Will reached toward him and found a hand. "It's okay. Really. I understand." Will set his wrap on his plate. "When we were finally getting our feet under us again, we moved from the car to a cheap, and I do mean cheap, trailer. It wasn't much larger than an RV. I hoarded food. I would save some of my lunch each day from school in case dinner wasn't possible."

"Did you ever have to eat it for dinner?"

"Once. But it wasn't anyone's fault. Mom missed getting to the bank and had to wait until the next day to cash a customer's check. She didn't hold checks, and told her customers that. Groceries were often paid for by those house cleaning checks. Dad's money was used to pay for the basics."

"How long did it take?"

"From car to trailer, to an apartment? About three and a half years. They have a small house now and live well below their means, spending what's necessary so emergencies aren't so tragic."

"What happened?"

"My father's company went bust and took all their employee owed incomes with them. Everything was sucked back into the company to pay fees and who knows what else. Now it's called vulture capitalism. Then it was known simply as robbery."

Parker flipped his hand beneath Will's and squeezed. "I'm glad they were able to get back on their feet."

"You will too," Will offered, holding on tight. "Give yourself time to readjust to the jungle out there."

"I'm trying." He dipped his chin, looking at his meal. "This means a lot to me, Will. Your friendship, all you are doing. Ian, Caleb. Even Summer. I'm starting to feel like me again."

"Well, I'm glad to hear it. I happen to like Parker quite a lot. The you who is Parker is a great guy."

After several minutes, they both went back to eating. Parker made a conscious effort to take his time and eat at a more relaxed pace and was glad when he felt he'd actually succeeded.

Chapter Thirteen

Parker was in Will's office about two weeks later for his promised cleaning. He greeted Tammie and was waiting for his appointment. He ignored the magazines. He'd already learned they were pointless for more than looking at pictures and seeing ads.

"Okay, Parker. He's ready."

He glanced up, expecting to see him, but only saw Tammie smiling at him encouragingly.

Parker walked through the waiting room door and into the hall, hunting for the right offset room.

"In here."

Following the voice, he spotted Will at the small service desk inside one of the exam rooms. "All ready for me?"

"Going to make you shine," he quipped. "Have a seat."

"Still edgy, just so you know."

"This is the stuff that shouldn't hurt at all. If something does, then there's a bigger problem. Hopefully we took care of all of them already."

"Hoping so." Parker wasn't so sure, but he wanted to trust Will. He did, a lot, but fear of the dentist was ingrained. He would almost prefer to be on a bull. *Almost.*

"Just relax."

In the few minutes it took to get him prepped, Tammie had joined them and they went to work. Will was very patient, explaining each step in the process and letting him see the tools he'd be using.

Out of nowhere, he got the distinct feeling Will would be so good with kids. He had that kind of temperament, that kind of patience.

It made him think of the rodeo and the day they'd unintentionally spent with Summer. That had been a good day, exhausting, and he'd really had fun with his honorary sister.

"Everything okay?"

He focused and realized he must have made a noise or something. He made a thumbs up sign.

"Almost done."

Good.

He closed his eyes and relaxed, letting him finish as memories floated through his mental viewer of that weekend.

The suction of the little pressure vacuum utterly disrupted his musings, but the next thing he heard was, "And you're done."

Woot!

He quietly clapped over his chest making them both laugh.

"Smart-aleck," Will chided playfully. Once he was cleaned up, Will said, "If you have a minute, I have a question. Well, more of a favor to ask."

"Sure. It'll be a few minutes before Ian can come get me, anyway." He sat up in the chair.

"Great. When you're done with Tammie, come into the office."

Parker settled up the bill, and got the adjusted balance. He hid his cringe. "I really need to get insurance." He'd talk to Ian and see what they did for him and the other two mechanics at the shop. He'd be paying on these bills forever.

Pocketing his receipt, he walked into the hall, taking an immediate turn into the office.

"What can I do for you?"

Will didn't look his way, tension making his shoulders bow in a little. "It's going to sound corny, but I've always believed things happen with a reason, in their own time."

"Okay."

Will was standing in front of the desk holding a couple of pages. "You know horses, right?"

"Been riding and working with them since I can remember."

Will handed over the sheets. "I want to go look at her, but I don't know one end from the other." He pointed to one of the chairs, and Will took its match. "I wasn't even planning on doing this right now, but one of my other patients has her. He said he has to sell her."

"Why?"

"His story is she's his dau—was his daughter's." He took a slow breath. Obviously the history behind the animal had gotten to Will. "His daughter passed away in May from a lung infection. That much I do know is true. I remember seeing her obituary in the newspaper. It's killing him to have the horse. No one rides her, and she's lonely."

"So, you don't even know if she's rideable?"

"He said she's a calm mare, but I have the same doubt. I don't want to buy her and find out after the fact that she's a hundred and ten and a menace to society."

Parker looked at the faxed pages. The mare's details were there, along with her history and pedigree. She looked sound on paper and in her photo, but he knew pictures could lie.

"I'll go with you to look, but remember, you won't want to buy her just because she's available. She might not be a good fit for you." When Will tilted his head in confusion, Parker added, "I'll explain it on the drive."

"Thank you." He stood. "I can call on Saturday."

He handed the pages over. "Sure. I'll be there."

Will smiled.

And Parker's heart tripped. Those smiles were going to drive him insane.

* * * *

Will tapped on Ian's front door Saturday morning. "All set?" he asked when Parker opened the door.

"Good to go." He leaned backward to shout into the house. "Caleb, I'm leaving." Will heard an answer and then they were in the car and gone.

Will got all kinds of information on the drive. Everything from personality to care and all the stuff in between.

Will held up a hand, stopping Parker in mid-lecture. "Are you sure you're not trying to convince me this is going to be a nightmare in the making?"

"No, well, maybe a little." Parker tapped his hat on his knee. "Just... People have personalities, dogs have them, cats, even horses. It could be oil and water. She might also be nothing but an expense that you have to feed and keep healthy."

"Would that be so bad?"

"No, but they are expensive pets."

Will could agree with that. "Okay, so let's say she's worth the effort, rideable or not. Is he asking a fair price?"

"For a decent age riding mare, you could probably negotiate out something more in your favor. For a twelve-hundred pound eating machine? No." Parker studied him. "Are you looking for something you can learn on?"

"I wasn't before this, but he made her sound like such a good, easygoing animal."

"Uh huh."

Will heard the distrust and doubt clearly. "You think he's overselling her?" They had spoken at length about the horse, and Will honestly hadn't asked a whole lot of questions. That was his own inexperience rearing its head, which was why he'd asked Parker to come along to see the mare.

"I think he found someone with a big heart, and a bigger bank account, who can pay him what he wants, not what she's worth. I'm worried he's playing you."

Will frowned, the shine of his Saturday adventures starting to lose its glow. Reality was a bitch. "I know I'm not experienced."

Parker touched his thigh. "I don't want him taking advantage of that. Don't tell him who I am, or what I've done. He may say something that will give me hints. Let him think I'm a friend for moral support. I'll even leave my hat in the car." He winked.

Will caught his hand and held on for a few seconds. "Thanks."

"I'll be fair, but I won't let him take advantage of you."

Will glanced across the seat. "Thank you. For coming and for being a friend."

Will followed the instructions in his hand, slowing when he spotted the mailbox beside the road. "Harkins. This is it."

He drove up to the house and stopped. "I'm nervous. Is that normal?"

"Don't be. He has to make the good impression on you. You just have to make him think you're sane for owning animals."

"This will be a first."

Parker touched his thigh again and then got out of the car. A man was coming through the front door. Will saw Parker unobtrusively slide his hat into the car.

"Mr. Harkins."

"Doc. Thanks for coming." They shook hands. "The barn's this way." All three rounded the house and aimed for the wide-roof, faded red barn. "Isis is eight or nine, like I said. Charlene rode her nearly every day."

"Is she calm enough for a beginner rider?" Will did know what his requirements were.

"She might not be right now because she's been under exercised but she doesn't spook easy."

Curiosity brought the horse forward in her stall.

"She is pretty," Will said. His rising hand faltered. "Will she bite?"

"No, but she can be pushy for treats. Carrots are her favorite."

Will nodded, reaching to pet her nose. She bumped him, looking for attention. Will sensed Parker behind his shoulder, quiet, observing.

"Let me put the halter on her and you can see her."

Will backed up a few paces. Mr. Harkins went into the stall and brought her out.

"Like I said, I'm willing to sell all her tack. I won't be riding anymore. My back can't take it. She deserves someone who will give her a good life and attention."

Will tried to remain objective. He watched the way she moved, looking for anything that might say otherwise to Mr. Harkin's story.

"Can my friend ride her for a few minutes?"

"I don't see why not." He handed over the rope and Will grasped it naturally. As he walked away, it hit Will.

He was *really* looking at this animal to buy her. To be her owner and take care of her.

"I'm insane," he mumbled. "I don't know one thing about horses."

"So you learn," Parker said quietly at his shoulder. "Let me take a look at her while he's not out here." Will nodded.

Parker ran hands over each leg, picking up feet for a few seconds. He tapped on the bottoms with the end of his pocketknife and then put them down. He walked behind her, a hand on her rump, to play with her tail once he was on the opposite side. He repeated the legs then looked in her mouth.

"She's the right age to what he's saying and she's calm. Let me see how she rides. She might be frisky to start if she hasn't been ridden lately, so don't let that surprise you."

"Parker..."

He met his gaze. "Second thoughts?"

"Terrified thoughts."

"If she's good, I won't lie, but if she's bad or too much, then you look again. That's all." He stood at the animal's head, scratching behind ears. "Are you serious about wanting to learn?"

"Yes."

Parker looked at Isis, then to Will. He hoped he wasn't about to say he couldn't teach Will what to do.

"Ask him how she is around other horses. That's important."

They turned around at the sound of footsteps. "Here's all her stuff. Could one of you help me? I can't lift that high with my back."

"I'll do it," Parker offered kindly.

"'Preciated."

Parker had her saddled in what seemed like seconds. "I'll only be a few minutes." He led her from the barn and Will and Mr. Harkins followed.

Will watched him hop on her like he had wings on his feet. She stood perfectly still, her head high. He leaned forward, talking to her and stroking her neck. Her ears flicked listening, then he tapped her and she moved with a good clip.

"She needs exercised, like I said, so she'll lose some of that roundness. Grass belly." He patted his gut. "Happens to all of us."

Watching Parker, he wanted to do that so badly. He'd watched all the riders at the rodeo, each one so graceful on their animals. Like they moved together, fluidly. He didn't have any fanciful notions. He needed to learn, but not since school had he wanted to try to learn something so out of the box for him.

He remembered to ask the question Parker had mentioned. Parker spent a few minutes having her make patterns and seeming to see how responsive she could be. He trotted up to them.

"She needs some of the spunk worked out of her system so she'll listen, but she's got a smooth gait and has a tender mouth."

"What does that mean?"

"She's responsive with a light hand. You don't have to control her like a wagon horse."

"Will you teach me?"

Parker blinked and looked down at him. He slid from the saddle. "Yes." He got close enough to whisper. "Haggle to drop a few hundred, with the tack."

"You sure she's good?"

He patted her neck. "I'll make you the kind of rider that she's perfect for."

Will gushed a sigh of relief. "I like her."

"Don't worry. You get her settled, and you'll be the next one on her."

Will gulped.

Not only had he decided to buy the horse, he also realized he was going to be spending a whole lot more time with Parker. He wasn't sure which made him more nervous—or more excited.

Chapter Fourteen

Parker found Will in the barn on a cooler Thursday evening. He was brushing down Isis in preparation for their lesson. She was a beauty of a mare, even among the horses boarding there. The more she grew accustomed to Will, the more confident he became around her. Her shiny bay coat was thickening for the coming winter. Parker had shown Will how to care for her feet, explained the importance of keeping her stall clean, and that no matter how bad his day went, or how bad the weather was, she had to be taken care of, fed, and watered. Will had dived into it, not one argument. Parker would see how he fared when the snow started falling. Or the next hard rain. The dentist was going to find out real fast just what he'd invested in.

He'd cowboy-ify his city slicker friend by spring, no problem. He'd already gotten Will into boots and jeans. Parker silently thought he was sexy with the new wardrobe and the swagger the boots seemed to naturally give him.

Ian had dropped him off after closing the auto shop and Will would get him home. He couldn't wait for his driver's license. Then he could see about finding a car. It would have to be something dirt cheap, but Ian wouldn't let him buy a bucket of bolts held together by good wishes and baling wire.

The license was one notch met, one thing he could check off his list of promises kept. It had felt so good too, holding the paper that said he passed the tests and he was worthy. He owed Caleb and Ian both for giving up their time and buckets of patience to teach him the rules and proper techniques. Especially Caleb. He was a stickler for doing it right. Of course, he was a cop. Couldn't get anything past him.

"Hey, Parker."

He smiled at the enthusiasm on his friend's face. "Ready for today?" Sunshine was broken by scurrying clouds as the winds started to change for the seasons. It was breezy and cooling. Great weather to get out on a horse.

Will nodded, his gray eyes sparkling as though they reflected fireworks. "I have a surprise for you." He set the brush in his hand to the side.

"You do?"

"Come here." He reached out a hand.

Parker saw it and balked, but accepted it, holding it firmly. Gratefully, Will didn't catch the slight hesitation. He couldn't help how he continued to feel himself reacting when he was close to Will. He'd been doing the best he could since the rodeo to keep it hidden. It hadn't been easy giving him lessons during the week, but their focus had been on his skills. Now that Will was gaining confidence, Parker wasn't sure what he could do to avoid the rapid beat of his heart whenever Will smiled at him.

"I've been talking to the boarders, seeing how they'd feel if I bought the property. The owner finally got city approval. I can buy it!"

"That's great." Will's excitement was contagious. He wanted to jump up and down with him and cheer, instead he gripped the hand in his in congratulations.

"I've told them I'm not changing their agreements and that the barn will still have boarding for them. They all take good care of it and their animals, so I really can't complain. At least this way the big thing gets used. Jerry is going to help keep track of the hay, since he's the one who usually gets here first to let everyone out in the morning."

Parker could tell how keyed up he was over the idea now that he had the city's approval. He was talking a mile a minute, which was so unlike the calm dentist Parker knew.

"Leslie has two geldings here. She asked if I knew anyone who could help her keep up with them past Christmas. She rides Buster as much as she can. I think that's her baby. But Tank is one too many." Will grinned wide. "I suggested you."

"She wants me to help exercise Tank?" Will let him go when they reached the stall. There were four boarders total, making six horses in the barn, including the newest, Isis. Parker had gotten into the habit of going around and petting them, saying hi if they were indoors. Often they were outside in the paddock. Today, there was one indoors, and that was where Will led him.

Parker leaned on the top rail and studied the gelding. A bright red sorrel, he looked to be in good health.

"You start today."

"I do?" Parker startled, gazing at Will.

"I want to ride with you. I know we won't go far." He gave him the pleading look that whether he knew it or not, rendered Parker spineless.

"You are doing well enough in the pen to try walking the pasture." He faced the animal and made noises to get him closer. Parker thought about it.

He'd love to be back on a horse, even if it was only a little and essentially a loaned animal. It was so very tempting. Will's skills were improving with each lesson, his hands and balance steadier. And he also silently wanted to do the same thing, ride with Will, share these afternoons together. They'd grown close over the last several weeks, very good friends. Parker knew he wouldn't say no. "Promise you'll tell me if something isn't comfortable." He petted the flat face, murmuring to him to get a feel for each other.

Will touched his arm and Parker twisted on his neck. The other man stood right at Parker's shoulder. Body heat ghosted over Parker's side. He hadn't realized Will was that close. His breathing snagged. His world faded. The only focus he had was Will. He leaned just a fraction, drawn in a way he'd never felt or known. It was impossible to fight the urge.

Will closed the gap before Parker's brain could catch up.

Searing heat rolled down his body with the first brush. It was sweet and soft and ultimately too short.

Will gazed at him, flicking to Parker's lips to rise again. "The only thing uncomfortable is how long I've been telling myself I don't want that."

Parker swallowed slowly. It hardly registered when Tank moved to his hay, leaving his hands empty. He shifted, facing Will. He cleared his throat when everything he wanted to say became lodged.

Will cupped the side of his head over an ear. "I've been fighting this for weeks." He sucked a breath that shook his frame. "I know you're still finding your way and you might leave tomorrow."

"I'm not leaving—"

Will shook his head, cutting him off. "I want to kiss you again. That's all I can think about. Now, at night, in the morning. I kept hoping you'd do it, let me know you wanted the same thing. I thought it was because you weren't interested, weren't ready but the more I've gotten to know you, the more I realized it had to be me first." Will held him immobilized, more by his words than his touch. "What your father did, what he said, is wrong. I finally figured it out. I've watched you and when you're around the horses, you are so free, you're incredible. You are free to be who you are, always." The silence in the barn went deep, like the world had stopped breathing. "I want to kiss you again."

Parker watched his own hand. It shook between them, and as light as a feather, he teased Will's bottom lip. "Haven't...long time," he finally managed.

"Have you been with other guys?"

"Sex. Not boyfriends."

Will nodded understandingly.

Parker felt the burning weight of Will's hand at his hip and almost whimpered. He'd been wanting this for so long, he nearly collapsed to the floor in shock when Will's lips found his. The kiss started slow, undemanding. Parker's eyes shut.

Somehow, he convinced his arms to move, winding them around Will's body. Will held him up, held him close. Will asked for a little more and Parker gave it, groaning when their chests pressed together.

Will echoed him, Parker feeling the quiet rumble rib to rib. He turned them both and braced Parker against the stall gate. He swore he'd forgotten how to move when Will finally released him. Both panted, neither separating quickly. Parker couldn't speak for Will, but he was a combination of mush and steel. He had absolutely no idea of what to do next.

Relief began to war with need when Will let a hand fall where he'd kept them so close. Parker wanted more. He just didn't know if the more he wanted was what Will wanted.

"We should probably..." Will tipped his head toward Isis, standing patiently with a knee cocked, half asleep.

Parker tried to make his brain work. He managed, "Does... Does Tank have gear?"

"In the tack room. Leslie showed me where it is. She said you're welcome to ride him as often as you want."

"Really?"

"She'd appreciate the help. She offered for me to do it, but I warned her I'm just learning. She said he can be a handful to start, which is why I thought of you."

Will reached for a hand and guided him to the tack room to point out the stored saddle and bridle. He also shocked Parker by giving him another slow kiss before moving aside to give him space. The first hadn't been an accident. And Parker was still trying to catch up.

"I've already got Isis' things. Saddle up, cowboy."

Thinking Will had left, Parker reached for the bridle, his brain barely computing the last several minutes. He'd never anticipated that kiss, or the ones that followed. The touch that happened in front of Tank's stall could have been dismissed, but not the ones after. He had to think Will wanted them as much as he did.

A hand on his butt made him gasp in surprise. "Will," he whined.

"Sorry." He took a step backwards. "I'm getting carried away."

"No! I mean, I love it." Parker grasped at him before he could run through the door and held his flat palm to his groin. "I can't ride with this."

"Oh!" Will's face flared red. "I didn't even think... I'm sorry."

Parker tugged him close, this time taking the initiative of the kiss. He didn't stretch it out, well aware he wasn't helping his predicament any. "Not mad. At all."

Gray eyes began to sparkle, losing their uncertainty. "If it helps, you're not alone." He sighed. "But you're right. Not the best time."

Parker brushed a light kiss this time. "Go. I'll be right there."

Will spun and vanished, for real this time. Parker sagged against an empty saddle stand, trying to gather the parts of himself Will had scattered out into the cosmos with those kisses. Something had clearly changed. What had Will seen? What had changed?

Parker had told him some of his history with his father, but there wasn't any reason to dredge up the darkest parts of his past. He was done with it. He would never be going back to Galveston.

"Find everything, Parker?"

He snapped to his feet, cobwebs leaving his thoughts. "Yeah, coming."

He looped the bridle and reins over a shoulder, slapped the saddle blanket on top of butt smoothed leather, and then hefted the western saddle off its brace. Nothing fancy, it only had to stay buckled and stay on.

Chapter Fifteen

A line had been crossed.

Will had tried for weeks to ignore the good things he continued to see in Parker. He'd lost count of how long he'd been playing this game. Through riding lessons, joking, and a friendship that was growing to mean more to him than just about anything. What he saw in the younger man was dedication to goals, ambition for his future. All the things Will had assumed about him, were wrong. He wasn't even sure when he'd given up denying how he felt.

Parker had been thrilled the day he'd passed his driver's test. Will knew he was on pace to get his GED. He was making a life for himself in a town that had adopted him. Ian's clan had opened up to him and taken him in, no questions asked. From what Will could see, Parker wasn't regretting their help in the least.

Will watched him remount Tank after opening the pasture gate to let them through. Part of the conversation he'd had with Leslie returned. Parker was good with all the horses, he seemed to understand them, the same way some people understood dogs. Leslie had been impressed with the progress he was making learning to ride Isis from Parker. Even six months ago, he wouldn't have imagined himself sitting on a horse, at least one not prompted by music with a pole up its spine.

Now he couldn't wait to get through his day, to spend time with Isis and Parker. If they rode, double fabulous. Even if they didn't, he was fine with that. He was waiting for the wonder of it to die down, but it hadn't. He knew colder weather would change things. Shorter sunlight hours. Snow. Bad weather stretches. Fascination could only last so long. He was beginning to think he'd been officially bitten by the bug and honestly, he didn't want to be cured.

The feel of sunlight on his face and warming his skin was divine. The scents of grass and nature on the breezes that blew over the open fields as they walked seemed to sink into him. Isis seemed to be enjoying the scenery change too, showing interest and looking around while walking with a firm stride. The other horses raised their heads on occasion to check them out, but otherwise, they couldn't be disturbed from their daily grazing.

Isis had lost weight just like Mr. Harkins said she would. She was toning up, and she wasn't the only one. After the first couple of weeks, stiffness faded from being astride and using muscles he never really had before. Hot showers had definitely been a necessity for a while but it was beginning to feel natural. Now he understood though why any rider had thigh and calf muscles of steel. Saddles only gave you something to cling to. The rest was up to the rider.

"Thank you, Parker."

"For what?" he replied absently. It seemed riding did lend itself to introspective thoughts for the both of them.

"Taking the time to do this."

He patted Tank's shoulder. "I've enjoyed doing it. I miss riding Chaser."

"Your horse?"

Parker sighed, sadness weighing him down. "I found out from Travis Dad sold him."

"Was he your horse or his?"

"He was mine in everything but name. He had the legal right."

"Well, that sucks."

"When you see Leslie, tell her thank you for me for loaning me Tank. He's a good animal."

"Do you like him?"

"Yeah. He's well trained. Just needs more exercise."

"That's what she said." He nudged Isis a little closer, side by side. It felt like she was responding better to him. Either he was getting better at his cues, or they were starting to get each other.

"How are you liking working at the auto shop?"

"It's okay. I've learned a lot."

"But..." Will prompted him.

Parker shook his head. "Not an engine guy. I promised Ian a year, and I won't break that. They've done too much for me."

A year? Will knew he didn't want Parker to leave. He didn't know what he was doing yet, what *they* were going to do, but he needed Parker there to figure it out. "What if you found something better suited?"

"All I know is horses and bulls, and I don't want to ride anymore. Travis almost lost his life," he said. "If I hadn't lost so much time and training, maybe, but not now."

"What were you thinking of doing after graduation? Before the fallout."

"After?" He stared forward, unblinking. "I guessed I would take over the ranch. Dad handled the business of it. I thought I'd take over and keep it running." He played with strands of the fiery red mane between his fingers. "Now? Really don't know."

The horses' easy plod allowed conversation to flow. They'd both settled into a relaxed pace as he and Parker walked along the fences of the pasture. The creak of leather and the scent of horse were becoming normal. The idea that he'd been baking since he'd received city approval to buy the Settler's estate, started to gain traction with the contemplative quiet.

"How well do you know computers?"

"Average, I guess. Why?"

"I have an idea that could work for both of us."

"Okay."

"When I made my case to buy the property, I said I wanted to do something that would help the community, and I meant that. Something that proved I meant a long-term investment in not only living here, but in Jasper. I want to make the boarding a profitable business, not just a rent intake."

"How do you mean?"

"Right now, they pay a flat fee for rent. Hay is delivered unless they have requests, so that's part of the rental expense they pay to me. I started migrating the business of it as soon as I heard I had approval. The sales contract for everything is already being drawn up. A lot of legality since the city is involved, the Heritage Committee... You get the idea. The problem is, I don't have the time to do a daily or even part-time job of running a boarding barn."

"You need a manager."

"I do. It's also a situation where I don't have time to teach someone the programs I'm already using, or the schedules I have for deliveries, things like that. I need someone who already has an idea of what running a barn takes." He had other ideas too, but waited to see how Parker felt about the ground floor ideas first.

There was the manual labor involved, the horses themselves, schedules, feeding, accessibility to owners. There was a lot of hands-on interaction, and that didn't even take into account the legal side of it with insurance, contracts... The list was long.

On top of taking over Dr. Kirkpatrick's practice, this was going to be more than he could handle, but the time was right to make the transition. Will didn't want to turn his back on the people who'd been renting space well before came onto the scene.

"So, what are you thinking?"

Will eased up on Isis' reins to stop. Parker did the same. "I want to offer you the job, if you're interested. If you're not bowled over and singing about working in an auto repair shop, that is."

"Me?"

"I've seen the way you are with the horses."

"I don't need a pity job, Will." Parker frowned. "I have a job."

Parker nudged at Tank. Will reached out then snapped his hand back when he felt his balance shift.

Parker must have seen part of it because he immediately brought Tank to him again. "Sorry."

Will centered himself and gripped the horn in front of him until his brain decided to listen, that he wasn't falling the five or so feet to the ground. "No, I know I'm okay. It just messed with my head. Let's walk," he said when he felt more in control. He tapped Isis lightly with a boot. "It's not a pity job. You have a job. A good one that is something you can fall back on if you want to continue in repair. This is a legitimate offer, with pay, of something that I know you love. You can't tell me you don't put your heart into horses."

Will had seen the depth of his sadness when he'd said his father had sold his own horse. Of how he'd been openly shocked hearing Leslie wanted his help with Tank. The truth was Parker missed horses.

If the horses didn't matter, their loss wouldn't hurt.

Parker adjusted his hat and twitched on his saddle. "Do you think you can trot?"

"Can't be any different out here than in the ring, right?

"Nope."

Will nodded and urged Isis into a faster gait.

"Heels down, back straight," Parker reminded him, keeping the same pace.

Will did, feeling the increased stretch of muscles. With the forward motion, they went longer than he usually would have in the pen. He watched the ground but still found himself relaxing into the gait.

When they reached one of the furthest fences, Parker slowed them down and turned around. "Let me think about it."

Will had hoped for an answer, but understood his reluctance. He had a little time before he had to openly search for someone. All he could do was hope it didn't come to that. It was one more added stress that he really didn't want to deal with.

When they returned to the barn, they bedded down Tank and Isis before gathering the other horses for their nighttime feed.

Once the chores were done, another thing Will had been thrust feet first into with buying the property, he walked up to Parker who was saying goodbye to Tank.

"I wanted you to know, the job isn't hinged on anything."

Unsure now with the job offer on the table, he was cautious to reach out and touch. Holding his hands at his sides, he realized he wanted to touch, badly.

"Like?"

Will rubbed his forehead. "I probably put the horse before the cart today." What happened in the barn before their ride had been pure instinct and desire. The job was common sense. Too bad the two weren't mutually inclusive.

Parker nodded. "I understand."

"You do?"

"The job is the important thing."

"That's not what I'm saying," Will argued.

Parker raised the brim of his hat. Will swore the more he saw of the man, the better looking he got.

"I don't need head games."

"That wasn't what I was..." He closed his eyes and sagged against wood. "I'm sorry. You're right. I'm not trying to confuse you." Christ, he was confusing himself. How could he not be causing Parker the same dilemma?

When he opened them, he startled. Parker had moved directly over him, had straddled his legs, and was framing his hands to the stall rail behind Will. He was pinned.

"Parker?"

"One is not dependent on the other, right?"

Will nodded, his heart racing against skin.

"So if I kiss you, the job offer is still there?"

"Yes," he whispered.

"And if I turn down the job, you'd kiss me, right now, right here?"

Will would probably do more than kiss him, but he got Parker's point. "I mean it."

Parker lifted his hat and hung it above Will's head. "I'll think about the job. I need to talk to Ian first."

"Tha..." He cleared his throat when he sounded scruffy. "That's fair." He understood Parker's rationales for it, even if his mind was misfiring in other directions with him so close.

"Ever been kissed in hay, Dr. Parkinson?"

"N— No." God, why couldn't he make his brain work? He didn't seem to have a whole lot of control with Parker staring at him like that.

Parker's hand slid into his hair and Will's body heated. The press of lips curled his toes. Both hands rose on their own and gripped at Parker's shoulders. For the first time, he got to find out just how strong Parker really was when he roped arms around his waist and hefted him into his body.

If Will had been startled by the position he'd found himself in, he was completely shocked by the move. After gliding a few feet, Parker set him on the ground and slowly urged him downward. Will heard the crisp crackle of the dried hay then felt it against his back, all the while Parker was kissing him. He licked at his top lip and nibbled at the bottom.

Teasing forays that continued mercilessly. They were driving Will mad with wanting.

"Parker."

Passionate kisses continued. Will had hoped it would feel good with Parker.

He hadn't expected this.

Chapter Sixteen

Parker locked his arms in the hay, hanging over Will who hadn't been able to catch his breath in several minutes. Turn about was fair play. Will had managed to completely derail Parker earlier in the tack room. It was his turn, and by the looks of things, he'd succeeded. He lowered to kiss and nip at Will's chin, hearing gasps and murmurs. The rough of stubble made his lips tingle. The faint scratch chin to chin was shooting arrows of desire into his blood.

Will dug hungry fingers into Parker's hair, holding him close.

He licked his way down Will's chin, relishing the flavor of sun-heated skin. He inched downward to tug the shirt he wore loose of his jeans. "Want to see you."

Will arched and Parker worked the shirt free, over his head to drop on the hay beside them. He didn't hesitate before moving in and worshiping.

Will whined his name. "Not fair."

Parker chuckled, licking in slow swirls over a nipple. "Oh?" Will was trembling beneath him. Coasting down his body, he nuzzled into the hard flesh behind denim. "I'm going to suck you."

"Fuck," Will choked.

"Not tonight."

Will groaned, the wanting clear in the sound.

"Do I need to cover you?" He really wanted to feel Will, feel him and taste him.

Will blinked, hazily focusing. "No. Clean."

Parker swept upward and snatched a hard kiss, burning with relief and need, then roamed south again. Like he was unwrapping a present, he separated fabric and moved it out of the way. His heart pounded with a needy tattoo into his ribs. He licked his lips when he found his prize, the gift in the package.

Parker hooked Will's jeans and moved them down below his rump. His hardened shaft popped upward to bob and rock with Will's harsh panting. Uncut and a good length, Parker craved him more. Will gripped it to tug and Parker eased his hand away.

"Patience," Parker suggested.

"Says you."

"That's right. Says me who is going to make you feel so good," he purred.

"How come..." He waved a hand, dropping it instantly for something to hold on to when Parker lowered his head to that delicious treat. Will never finished the thought. Gripping at Parker's shoulder, he moaned thickly. "Parker. Hell!" His head snapped backward on his neck when Parker took the flat tip between his lips.

The same tortured licks he'd given to his nipples were repeated, earning even more of a reaction. Parker was taking his time, drawing it out, and the unhurried pace was driving Will insane.

The last time he'd had sex, it had been a necessity. This was all for pleasure, Will's and his. And he was definitely loving it. He fell into a rhythm, slow and deep. Will's grip flexed on his shoulder, his chest heaving.

Stretching out beside him on the hay, he found Will's sac, rolling the jewels in his palm. He moaned loudly, making Parker smile. Will wasn't a quiet lover. After clandestine and secret fucks in the shadows, he liked that. A lot.

Stretching his fingers, he caressed flesh, almost but not quite reaching his entrance. Will was riding the edge. Drops hit Parker's tongue with Will's unique flavor.

"Fuck!" Will lurched, thrusting into his mouth.

Sucking deeper, Parker let him find his zone, stroking and teasing with fingers, tongue, and teeth.

"Parker!"

Adding a hint of pressure with daring fingertips did it. The flesh between his lips pulsed, and a jet of fluid hit his throat. He glided upward to catch it, milking him dry. As the final jerks tickled his tongue, he petted Will's stomach, bringing him back to earth.

"Ho-*ly* hell," Will panted, lying limp in the hay.

Small shocks rolled over him as muscles flexed beneath Parker. Licking him gently, he found any lingering drops, catching his own breath as his heart calmed. Light fingers sifted into his hair, combing it with tender strength. "That was..." Will sighed.

Parker smiled, hiding it. *No words.* He shivered as zaps of energy struck nerves, coming down off the edge himself.

"What about you?" Will asked.

"I want to get tested first."

"Do you think you—?"

Parker popped up and kissed him, cutting him off. "No. It's been almost a year, and I feel fine. I never went without protection, but that's all beside the point. I'm not an idiot. You're low risk for me. I can't say the same." He frowned. "I'm sorry." He shouldn't have presumed, should've said something to give Will an out if he'd wanted it. Guilt slammed into him. He went to move away, but Will made a grab for his shirt and yanked him down.

"What can I do for you?" Earnest eyes bore into him. "I'm not going to be selfish." He threaded into Parker's hair again. "Love this. Love playing with it."

Parker smiled softly, closing his eyes to enjoy the strokes. Relieved, he sank to Will's shoulder. A moment later, Will reached and pulled up his jeans.

"Hay is prickly."

Parker laughed in understanding, giving him a hand to cover exposed skin, then they settled down.

"This is all you want?"

Parker dropped an arm over Will's bare waist, pressing into his shoulder to nuzzle his throat. "Just this." Parker didn't know the last time he'd simply been held.

* * * *

Will roamed his spine with a light hand, curled up together in the hay. He felt the tautness of Parker's groin pressed against his hip but he made no requests, and Will wasn't going to force it. The hay scratched at his back, but he could handle that. His eyelids drifted closed while floating in the aftermath.

It was growing dark, the sun setting as the earlier evenings and shorter days became more noticeable. Lights through the barn kept most of the shadows at bay. Soon they'd have to get up to shut doors and check water one last time. *Just not yet.* He hadn't felt this relaxed in a long time. Will hadn't held anyone in his arms like this in a long time, either.

Roy had been... He counted backward. Two years ago? Nearly three now, he supposed. He'd been on dates, but the area of Daytona where he'd lived hadn't been gay-friendly. Most of the men he came across were in the closet or weren't interested in more than sex. He was almost positive a few he'd met over drinks had been married. It was discouraging to say the least.

Granted, Will wasn't in a hurry to settle down, but he needed stability. Needed to trust the person he was emotionally tied to. And he wasn't a fan of sex just because. Like Parker feared, there were consequences. Plus he had health requirements to adhere to, that any slip could potentially endanger his patients was unacceptable. He refused to take that kind of a chance, so he understood Parker's reticence. He also admired his maturity to make that stand and not feel neglected, but more so, to be worried about Will's reaction.

He cuddled Parker closer, nuzzling the top of Parker's head with his chin.

"I should probably get going. Ian's going to worry if I don't."

"Okay." He followed with his gaze as Parker started to rise. "I'll take you home." Parker dusted himself off, then offered a hand. Grasping his shirt first, he clasped Parker's palm to be hauled to his feet. "I had no idea you were that strong."

"Never been shy about hard work."

"You're a good man, Parker." Will caught him by the waist and kissed him, almost instantly creating a fresh wave of longing he wished he could continue. He let go, breathing harder. "Right. Home."

Parker smirked and reached for his hat off the tie-down hook. He brushed his hair behind his ears and put it on his head. He whispered after Will finished putting on his shirt, "I like you too." Parker licked beneath Will's ear. "A lot," he added.

Will shivered with lust. "Home. Now. Or you're going to be *really* late, and I'll have no way to explain it and look Ian in the eye."

With a wave from inside the car, he waited until Parker was walking through the door before driving away. Not even a minute later, his cell phone rang. It was Ian's number. It surprised him that his hand trembled a little gripping it.

"Hello?"

"Ian asked me to invite you to Sunday breakfast." It was Parker. The guy really needed a phone. For a heartbeat, he'd thought it *was* Ian and he was in tons of trouble, imagined or otherwise.

Will let out a slow breath, hoping he sounded calmer than he felt. "I'd like that."

"This is their weekend, so here at ten."

"That works."

"Hold on a second." Will heard background noise fade. "Can I call you in a little while?" Parker had lowered his voice.

"Of course."

"Ever have phone sex?"

Will choked and Parker's laugh grew sultry, leaning into evil territory.

"I'll take that as a no. You sounded so good earlier." His breathing was growing raspy. Will imagined he was rubbing his hand over his package. He'd love to see that. "I didn't get to finish."

"I offered," Will immediately replied. He tried to keep his attention on the road, going a little slower than the speed limit. Parker wasn't making it easy for him.

"I know, but this is safer until I know it's okay. First thing Monday I'll go. There has to be some place around here I can get it done." His tone changed. "I'll call before bed. I want to talk to Ian before he goes."

"All right." He let out a slow breath. The seducing tease was gone. The TV was in the background again.

"Talk in a bit. Bye."

"Bye." Will hung up the call, carefully putting the phone down. He dropped a quick peek at his crotch, and shook his head. He'd come less than an hour before, and the man had managed to get him hard again. Over the phone, with just his voice.

He pushed into the seat, gripping the steering wheel in stiff arms on the drive home, fighting the ache, and losing.

Chapter Seventeen

Ian was cooking breakfast the next morning while Caleb was in the shower. Sundays were some of the best days in Parker's book, but he understood the undertaking it was to feed so many people. He helped prepare the table and stack plates on the counter out of the way for when they'd be needed. In the months Parker had been living there, he'd learned where he could help Ian, who did the bulk of the cooking, so Caleb could grab a little extra sleep. The kitchen smelled awesome with maple sausage, bacon, and chunky potatoes. Home cooked just couldn't be beat.

Parker really wanted to talk to Ian about Will's offer. He was nervous, though. Ian had done so much for him. Both Ian and Caleb. Where would he have been if they hadn't stopped four months ago? If they'd pushed him away? If they'd walked right by him like he had been invisible when so many had? Not only would he still be out there, he would have missed the chance to reconnect with Travis. He would have missed Will.

He probably would have died.

Which was why he felt so low for wanting to accept the job. He hated feeling indebted.

"Something on your mind?" Ian whisked eggs in a bowl. Biscuits waited in tins to go into the oven with the first arrivals. It had all become a well-timed process.

Parker blinked, swallowing to find his voice. "How do you do that?"

Ian arched an eyebrow. "Old man talent."

Parker nudged his shoulder. "Shut up." He drew a deep, deep breath. "You said until I found my next road."

"I did."

"Will offered me a job as his barn manager." He tensed, waiting for the explosion, the physical. A sign.

Ian's whisk didn't so much as skip a beat.

"What does a barn manager do?" he asked curiously.

Parker gave an abbreviated explanation.

"And you want to do it?"

"I don't want to make you mad," he whispered.

The whisk slowed, then Ian settled it in the bowl. Turning, he tugged on Parker's shoulder to face Ian. "That wasn't what I asked. Is the job something you feel stronger about than pushing a bristle broom and checking waste volumes?"

Parker started to shake his head.

"Don't lie, Parker," Ian said quietly but firmly. "This isn't me. This is you. What you want."

"Would I still live here?"

"Does the job come with a room?"

"Not that I know of."

"The job and the room here are not tied together, if that is what you're worried about."

Parker lowered his gaze. "You've done so much..."

"And you've worked hard and paid for what you owe me." Ian sighed slowly. "Let me guess. Your father had stipulations."

"On everything. Conditions to be able to ride. Rules to how often I could take off."

"We're treating you like an adult. I want you to understand that your decisions will always have consequences, but you will never have to bargain for them."

Parker's eyes widened when Caleb joined them, moving into Ian's side. What he expected was not what he heard, though.

"He's right, son. Do you really think we would have put up with anyone who abuses and cheats? Given any person the opportunities we have given to you if you hadn't earned them?" Caleb wrapped an arm around Ian's waist. "You've made mistakes and nothing exploded. We've made mistakes with you and the world didn't crack."

"I have?" That shocked Parker. He'd been trying so hard...

Caleb chuckled. "See? We all made them, we talked or corrected it and whatever it was, was so uneventful, that you can't recall them."

Parker didn't know what to say.

"We're not going to ever raise a hand against you, son," Caleb said solemnly. "Ever."

Parker's breathing hitched as he fought for control. How he'd ever been so lucky to find these two, he'd never know, and he knew better than to question. "I want the job."

"So long as you make enough to pay for the room, and whatever you want above that, you're still welcome here."

Ian released his husband to return to the eggs. People were going to be arriving any minute.

"The only problem is I don't have a car."

Parker saw Caleb and Ian share a look, and a single nod between them. He swore they could read each other's minds.

"Do you think you'll make enough for a car payment?" Caleb asked.

Parker didn't know. "We haven't talked about that yet."

"Go ahead and find out. I have a suggestion or two."

"You do?"

Caleb nodded. The first knock of the morning echoed through the house. "Why don't you go let in the masses? They're going to be hungry."

Dazed, Parker did as Caleb asked. He found Brice and Jake. "Morning." They came in, but Parker stayed at the door. Jeannie, Wanda, and Summer were walking up.

* * * *

Will pulled up to the side of the road in front of the house behind one of the trucks. He was nervous, being with such a large group. When another car pulled up behind his, he guessed it was time to stop sitting there like a bump on a log staring across the yard.

He joined the pair walking up to the door.

"Hi." The guy offered a hand. "Tucker and this is Vivian."

"Will."

That was all he got to say because the door opened when they hit the steps. "Morning guys," Parker said, smiling broadly, his eyes twinkling in the sunlight. Then those eyes lit on Will and his heart beat fiercely in reaction. "Hello, to you," he all but purred against Will's ear. Will bit his lip to not groan. "Let me introduce you." He shut the door.

Dutifully, Will followed as he met Caleb and the others. He recognized Ian and got a wave from in front of the stove.

"Is this everyone?" Caleb called.

"Yes," someone replied.

Caleb clapped his hands together. "Okay, then. Dig in!"

"Just grab a plate and follow the masses," Parker suggested. "Count your fingers when you're done."

"Hey!" someone grumbled. "I heard that."

"You're the one who dared to sword fight over the last biscuit," someone else—one of women— countered. Snickers echoed behind Will. "Don't mess with a girl who has four brothers." He wondered if it was Vivian. She didn't sound like Summer's moms.

He filled his plate, amazed at the amount of food, but could guess with that many, and the majority of them men, there wouldn't be much left. He followed Parker and sat down, waiting until everyone joined them.

"Wow," Will breathed taking in the group as everyone took a seat. "Every week?"

"Every Sunday, at a different house. It's fun, and gets everyone together."

"How long have they been doing this?"

"Going on four years now," Brice said from Parker's other side.

"How did it start?"

"Not long after Jake and I got married, we invited everyone to breakfast at our house, and it snowballed from there."

"I came into it about two years ago," Vivian said from across the table. She leaned over her plate. "Run. Run while you can." It was dire, but her eyes were glimmering so much, Will knew she was clowning around.

It was insane, loud, boisterous, and so unlike anything Will could remember. Laughter, teasing, loving looks, and affection were visible and heard in every direction.

"Vivian, are you feeling okay?"

Will glanced toward her and noticed she was looking a little off. She pushed her plate forward.

"Yeah, I'm fine. The eggs aren't agreeing with me. I'll be okay in a few minutes."

Only she wasn't. She slipped from her chair and made a dash for the hallway.

"Be right back." Wearing a concerned frown, Tucker stood and went to find his wife.

"It's not your eggs, Ian," Jake pointed out, stuffing his face. Light laughter followed his attempt to ease worry from around the table.

Everyone waited to see what had happened.

Vivian returned a few minutes later with an attentive Tucker at her elbow. She took her seat and began to nibble on a biscuit.

"Everything okay?" Wanda asked.

"I'm pregnant."

Bombshell.

One of the *loudest* whoops Will had ever heard in his life erupted. "Congratulations!" Everyone raised a glass in toast.

"Thanks guys," she said, starting to sound a little steadier and more relaxed. "Can't hide it when stuff like that happens."

"Oh?" Will asked.

"We wanted to wait another two to three weeks to make sure there wouldn't be problems."

"Can't always do that," Jeannie said in commiseration.

"Nope," Vivian agreed.

"So, I talked to Ian."

Will focused to his side, letting Parker know he had his attention while everyone else talked baby stuff.

"I want the job. I need to know what you thought the pay would be."

Will smiled. He hadn't realized how relieved he would be that Parker would want to take it. "What are you making now?"

They began to talk numbers, confirming what Will expected from the business side of it and where Parker could improvise to streamline the process.

"Still something you want to take on? It's going to be monotonous, and hard labor."

Parker shrugged. "It's what I know, something I thought I'd always be around."

Will was glad for his pragmatism. "Then you're hired. You can start as soon as you get it cleared to leave the auto shop."

The phone rang, and Ian stood from the table to answer it.

"Parker, it's for you."

"Huh. For me?" he whispered. He shrugged at Will's questioning stare. "No idea."

He stood from the table and grasped the phone, going around the corner to hear. It was pretty loud around the table.

When he didn't return for several minutes, Will began to worry. Who would be calling him? Wasn't everyone he knew sitting at that table?

Brice leaned over Parker's empty seat. "Why don't you go see what's keeping him? Around the wall to the right. If he's in his room, it's the second door on the right."

That was all the push he needed. The confused worry must have been fairly obvious.

"Excuse me?" He placed his fork by his plate and stood. He knew several watched him, but he really didn't care. All that mattered was finding Parker and knowing he was all right.

Following Brice's directions, he found Parker sitting on a bed in a bedroom. "Everything okay?"

He shrugged a shoulder. He was clearly upset about something.

Will sat beside him.

Parker rolled the cordless phone in his hands. "That was Travis. My father had a heart attack this morning."

"Is he..."

"He died."

Knowing what he did, Will wasn't sure what Parker wanted or needed. He waited in silence.

"I didn't want to ruin their morning."

"What are you going to do?"

"I have to go..." A shaky breath rocked him. "It's not home. Not anymore, but I have to go."

Will put an arm around his shoulder. Parker twisted and buried himself in Will's neck.

Chapter Eighteen

Parker was on a bus Tuesday morning for the long, overnight drive. He'd arranged for Travis to pick him up at the east Houston station Wednesday. All he wanted to do was get everything over with and get home to Jasper. Get home to Will.

Galveston felt foreign now.

He stared unseeing out the truck window as they traveled the country roads to the ranch. It looked foreign, too. Winter dryness had hit the fields, turning them golden yellow, or they simply lay fallow, barren and dark waiting for spring planting. Trees that far south were showing changes when the trees at home were weeks ahead in their color explosions.

Not much was said on the drive. Parker hoped Travis understood his apathy. He wouldn't be there if there wasn't a legal obligation.

Travis walked with him inside the house when they arrived. Parker left his bag by the door. He didn't know what he was going to do now that he was back.

Not much had changed in four years. The living room looked the same. Same TV, same furniture. Same, but not. It felt different. It didn't feel welcoming any longer. It felt...cold. He was a stranger in this house now.

"Travis? That you?"

"Yeah, Kyle."

"Kyle?" Parker asked. "Really?"

"Yeah, he's your dad's foreman now." He scuffed a step. "Well, was. Now he's yours."

Okay, he was wrong. A lot had changed. Kyle had been on the ranch for about a year before Parker had been kicked off it, but Dawson had been the foreman. "Where's Dawson?"

"He's working for me now."

"Really?"

"He didn't care for what your father had done to you and they fought. Dad took him on, and when Dad died, I promoted him to handling the herd."

"Parker?" Kyle froze across the room like he'd seen a ghost.

"Hey."

Kyle rushed him and swept him into the hardest bear hug. "Fuck a duck! You're home! You're alive!"

"I didn't lie, Kyle," Travis joked.

"Had to see him with him with my own eyes. Has Dawson seen you? Has any of the guys—"

"No, just you, Travis, and Eddie."

"Your dad told everyone you'd done run off."

Parker rolled his eyes. "And everyone believed him."

"Course not! But he was the boss." Kyle bowed his head. "None of us knew what he'd done for days. Dawson suspected, they fought, your daddy fired him and no one asked again."

Parker nodded. "It's okay." It wasn't less than he'd expected. He was just as sure the old fucker hadn't had the balls to tell them *why* he'd thrown out his only son, either.

"Let's get something to drink. The lawyer will be here in a few hours to go over the will."

"Already?" Parker was drained after being on the bus for a full twenty-four hours. There was still the funeral to deal with. All he wanted was Will. There was absolutely nothing in that house, on that land, that Parker needed or wanted more.

"She wanted to get it done as soon as she knew you were alive and could come home to take care of the details."

"Fuck," Parker muttered. "That's all right. Faster I can get home."

"But you are home." Both Travis and Kyle gaped at him. "And you don't have to leave again, ever," Kyle pointed out.

"I'm not staying. I'm sorry."

Kyle's face fell. "But... The ranch."

"I'll probably put it up for sale." He hadn't thought about it much yet. "I'm sorry, Kyle."

Travis shrugged when Kyle glanced in his direction. He then dropped a glare at Parker. "Maybe you shoulda stayed gone then. I'm not losing my job because you don't give a shit about this ranch."

"Get out." Parker went to walk around him.

"What? You going to waltz in here and fuck up the whole damn ranch because you don't give a shit? I'm calling you on it, Parker! You're back five fucking minutes and already being a dick!"

"I said, get out," he repeated without raising his voice, walking away. "I'm exhausted. You don't know shit."

Parker heard Kyle ranting to Travis, but he really didn't care. He didn't want anyone jumping all over him for making hard decisions.

He heard the front door slam. Travis joined Parker a few minutes later in the kitchen.

"Are you staying to meet with the lawyer with me?" He poured water from a jug in the fridge, the same way he had for most of his life.

"If you want me to."

"I'd like it if you could. When is the funeral?" He assumed by this point, it was already handled.

"Saturday."

"Fine." He could be gone by Monday.

Travis found a glass and did the same thing. "You're really not planning on staying?"

"No. I have a job, a roof, and I hope a boyfriend back home."

"But this is your home," Travis argued.

Parker ran a hand down his face and sagged against the counter. He popped off his hat and rested it by the sink to scrub a hand through his hair. He never did cut it once he found out Will liked it longer. "No, it's not. It's the house I grew up in. It's also the house I was thrown out of."

"And no one can do that again." He leaned next to Parker. "Look, just see what the lawyer says before you go hell bent on selling the place, okay? There's four men who work the ranch for your dad. Kyle has done a damn good job with the breeding and the livestock."

Parker didn't want to argue. "Fine, I'll listen, but I'm not making any promises."

Travis sipped at his water. "You've changed," he said.

"So have you."

"Have you changed so much though that you don't want what you've always wanted since you were able to ride a horse?"

Parker stared into his water. "I have, Travis." He sighed, knowing his friend would never understand because they didn't walk the same road. "I've found..." Parker stopped. How could he explain he had a family now? Friends who'd been there for him?

Family he adored even if they weren't blood? How could he describe what he had now? "Tell me something. Do you and Eddie live together?"

"No."

He honestly hadn't expected that. He'd thought for sure they would be living together after what he'd seen at the rodeo. "Why not? You travel together, you obviously love each other."

"Because..."

Travis didn't finish it.

"That's why I'm not staying," he explained gently. It wasn't the example he'd hoped to make, yet this was an even stronger one. "I don't have to make excuses, hide, or lie, to anyone, over anything. You're living the best way you know how, but I bet you and Eddie would be so much happier if what I saw on the road, existed here, too."

"I'd lose men."

"Then you find men who respect you for who you are, not who you sleep with." He drained his glass. "Ask Eddie how he sees it. I bet he'd jump at the chance to really be with the man he loves." He grabbed his hat in a hand. "I have that at home. I can be me. No one calls me names. No one threatens my life. And I think I love the man who is waiting for me." He met Travis' troubled stare. "I'm sorry. This is over for me. I'll do the best for the men here and the ranch, but it's not my life anymore. Now, I'm going to go change out of these clothes and clean up." It wasn't as pleasurable as it sounded. He didn't even know what of his room remained.

"Okay."

"I'm still your friend. I'm just not the boy I was any longer."

"You're a much better man than I've been."

"No, I'm just the man I'm supposed to be right now."

Travis snorted. "Now you sound like Eddie."

"See? You miss him. Go call him. I need time to take a shower." Parker wanted to take a few minutes to call home himself.

Travis nodded, drained his water, and then walked out of the kitchen. Parker listened for him until he heard the front door close. He didn't hear the truck start, so he knew his friend hadn't left. Sometimes what a man needed to say needed to be said in private.

* * * *

Parker showered and changed. He called home and to Will's, leaving messages that he'd arrived and would call again that evening when he knew more. Travis met up with him inside about twenty minutes before an unknown car pulled in front of the house under the thinning oak trees. A woman found her feet at the side and reached inward to reappear with a briefcase.

"Mrs. Adams." Parker held out his hand and greeted her when she reached the door.

"It's good to meet you, Mr. Vandersoot." Her grip was firm but not hard. "Is everyone here?"

"Travis and me. I asked him to be here."

"That's fine. Is there a Kyle Steppen still on property?" She settled her case on the kitchen table.

"I think so."

"He's listed on the documents."

"Let me go see if he's out in the barn." Travis left the kitchen in search of Kyle.

"Something to drink?" There wasn't much, but he knew it was rude to not offer.

"No, I'm fine. Thank you." She pulled out a seat. "Why don't we chat a little before they return?"

Parker pulled out a seat across from her.

"Your father rewrote the will about three years ago."

That shocked Parker. "I didn't know. He kicked me out right before my seventeenth birthday. This is the first I've been here in four years."

"I'm sorry to hear that." She frowned. "You didn't leave by your own choice?"

"No, ma'am."

"And you were still a minor?"

"Yes, ma'am."

She cupped her hands together. "Can others confirm that?"

"At least two. Dawson, Dad's old foreman, and Travis. I believe others suspected, but didn't want to risk their jobs by confronting him."

"That leaves an opening for you, then." They both heard the door open. "We'll talk more after. I'm sure you're going to have questions."

Travis sat at the table as did Kyle, only he took a further chair, glaring at Parker. For the most part, he ignored the guy.

Placing the pages on the table, she said, "Okay, let's get started, shall we?"

As she read through the pages, it became immediately clear why she said he'd have questions.

His father had left the whole fucking ranch, the beef business, the hay fields, everything—to Kyle.

About halfway through it, Kyle seemed to get the idea of the momentous lottery win that had fallen into his lap and jumped from his chair. "Get off my fucking ranch!"

"Please, Mr. Steppen," Mrs. Adams said.

"It's mine! He gave it to me and not his dick loving son!" He fist-pumped the air.

She arched an eyebrow. "Really? So there's cause for discrimination, as well?"

Parker didn't get to answer. Mrs. Adams did the best third grade, *you're in trouble* voice Parker had heard in years. "Mr. Steppen. Sit. Down."

Kyle did, glaring at Parker boldly.

"Now then. The ranch is not legally yours until all the deeds and paperwork have been filed."

That seemed to take some of the wind out of Kyle's sails. "But... I'm the one who's been runnin' it."

"That's not in question." She tamped down pages. She caught Parker's gaze. "Why don't you come to my office tomorrow, and we'll discuss your options."

At first, there had been a jolt of elation. Parker could get the ranch! But the second he heard Kyle's gleeful hate, he remembered he had a better place, and a better man, waiting for him. He stood from the table with her.

"Mrs. Adams. I won't be contesting the will. You can sign everything under the sun over to Kyle. I'm not staying where I'm hated."

"Are you sure, Mr. Vandersoot? There's a lot of money tied up in this enterprise."

"I've been without money for four years. Until very recently, I'd been without family. My family is waiting for me back home." Immediately, images of a laughing Summer and the mayhem of Sunday morning breakfast entered his thoughts. "The only person I have here is Travis, and I won't be losing him twice."

He put a hand on Travis' shoulder. He understood the disappointed sadness in his eyes, but he couldn't live his life for Travis.

"How does a gay boy have a family?" Kyle sneered.

"Might I add, until the documents are filed, Mr. Vandersoot does still own this property, and has the rights of heir of ownership to handle it as such."

"What does that mean?" Kyle snapped.

"It means," she sniped with just enough force to make her point, "you're insulting your boss until the county stamps the deed. And I can guarantee both myself *and my wife* will be sure to spread your sentiments around the county. You'll never have a buyer within a thousand miles again."

Parker bit his lip to hide his laughter as Kyle got the meaning of that last slap of reality.

"If you can't learn humility, you'd better learn tolerance." She walked to the end of the table, her short heels making a crisp snap that echoed her warning, effectively ignoring Kyle from then on. "It's been a pleasure, Mr. Vandersoot. Come by my office at your convenience after tomorrow morning to finalize the transfer without claim. I sincerely hope your future is bright."

"It is." He smiled, hiding nothing. He knew there was nothing there in Galveston that could hold a candle to what he had at home.

"Goodbye, Mr. Hopeck. Thank you for being here." She shook and then left.

The silence lengthened awkwardly. Parker finally broke it. "I'm not staying, Kyle, but she does have a point. Gay or not, you have a business to run."

Travis had something to say, too. The rough gravel of his voice sounded heavier. He was pissed at Kyle, and Parker loved him more for the support. "If you ever, and I mean *ever* want to work with my spread again, you will learn tolerance."

"But you're not—"

Travis rolled his eyes.

"Are you fucking serious?"

"It's because of people like you that I've been hiding my life." He faced Parker. "And it's because of people like him that I'm not going to do it anymore. So get over it."

"It'll all be yours in a matter of days." Parker knew he wasn't staying longer than he had to. "The sales, the herd, the taxes. Have fun with it."

"I'll never let another faggot on this land." Kyle was glaring again, like a rabid dog with a target.

"That's your choice," Travis said. "You want to come stay with me? I've just officially broken off all business here."

"I don't need it!"

"Better check those books," Travis suggested. "Parker's dad and my dad were in business together for more than twenty years. You're going to need to find new suppliers for breeding bulls and calves."

Parker palmed his pack and snatched his jacket and hat off hooks by the door. "Ready when you are."

Oddly, or maybe not, Parker didn't feel a thing watching his old house vanish for the last time in the side view mirror.

Chapter Nineteen

Will cautiously closed the door to the rental car. After the welcome he'd just... No, that had been no welcome. He sincerely hoped he had the right place this time. The asswipe at what he'd *thought* had been Parker's spread hadn't been the most forward with information. He had been a sneering asshole.

He pulled the light jacket closed, glad he'd thought to not pack it in his suitcase. Leaving the travel bag on the car's rear seat for now, he walked up the wooden steps, trying to make it look like he was supposed to be there, and knocked when he reached the door.

"Is this the Hopeck ranch?" he asked the young woman who answered the door.

"Yes. Come in." She closed the door. "How can I help you?"

"Uh... I'm looking for Parker Vandersoot."

Her expression cooled. "Are you a friend of Kyle's?"

"No."

That seemed to be the right answer. She lost the stiffness in her demeanor instantly. "Let me hang up your jacket. Something hot to drink? He's in the pastures with Travis. I need to radio to them."

"That would be very kind." He held out his hand. "I'm Will Parkinson."

"Parker's Will?" Her dark eyes began to dance.

Will smiled. *Parker's Will.* He liked the way that sounded. "I suppose."

She took his hand and clasped it between hers. "I'm pleased to meet you. I'm Marta Flores, Eddie's sister. We're here for the holiday, and the boys are out checking cattle to be tagged. He's been talking about you nonstop for two days."

The butterflies Will had harbored about making this trip unannounced and very impulsively began to calm. "I thought he'd be at his own place."

She frowned. "Parker can explain it. He signed the pages this afternoon. That *pendejo* can have it!"

Parker had explained some of it before he'd left for Texas, but Will had a feeling he'd neglected to mention all of it after running into the anti-welcoming committee already.

He followed her into the kitchen. The enticing scents of spicy cooking and corn bread made his mouth water. A big pot on the stove seemed to be the origin. He sniffed.

"*Menudo.* It's good after a day in the chill. One of Eddie's favorites." She reached for a walkie-talkie on the counter. "Base to herd."

"Go ahead base." Will recognized Travis' voice.

"Tell *chulo papi* he has company. *Muy guapo.*" She released the button, grinning like a woman with a secret, and winked. "I'm guessing this is a surprise for him."

Will nodded. "The funeral is tomorrow." And he missed Parker.

"I don't know why he insists he has to go. *Cabrón.* He hurt Parker, and I didn't even know him." She crossed her arms, scowling.

"Herd to base. Parker's on his way."

She raised the handheld to speak. "*Gracías.* Don't forget, dinner in two hours."

"*Gracías*, Marta. You're a good sis." That was Eddie.

"And don't think I'll ever let you forget it." She placed the talkie on its charger bed. Smiling broadly, she said, "He'll be a few minutes. What would you like to drink?"

At least he could hope Parker took his surprise visit as well.

* * * *

Parker loped across the pasture on one of Travis' work geldings, wondering who could be there to see him. The only people he cared to talk to were on this ranch. He'd spent an hour and a half at Mrs. Adams' office that afternoon signing away his claims to what had once been his home. *Once, a long time ago.* Just like a blood relation could contest a will they wanted to challenge, he was forgoing the right to make that challenge, which was where all the signing came into play. He'd never set foot on that land again. He had no need for it. Doing a search through the house had proven if there was anything of his personal life there, it was well hidden. His room had been stripped, his memories, gone. Whatever he needed he'd have to handle himself.

Thankfully, with Caleb's help, he'd already received copies of his birth certificate and social security card in the months he'd been living with them. The less he needed from that time in his life, the better.

There was a very wicked gleam in the lawyer's eyes while they went over each page in meticulous explanation.

She'd made a copy of the packet for him, and while shaking his hand goodbye said, "Don't worry, Mr. Vandersoot. You are free and clear of all responsibility from the property, the livestock, and the taxes."

"Should I be worried?" That sounded ominous.

She smirked. "Not now. The tax assessor will have a few things to discuss with Mr. Steppen, however."

"He's not the one who deserves to be raked over the coals."

She considered him, and nodded. "I understand. You're a forgiving, young man."

"Other than being an idiot, he was an all right guy." What else could he say? He'd had no idea Kyle was a bigot before Wednesday. Before he'd become a ghost, they'd been nothing to each other. That seemed to be the way it was going to remain.

She saw him out of the offices and once he'd returned to Travis', he'd saddled Sand Bar's Mission, AKA Sandy, and had hunted down Travis and Eddie. A few hours in the saddle had swept the first half of his day out of his thoughts. And he'd be going home on Sunday. Back to Will. He couldn't put it to words how much he missed Will.

After being there for most of the week, he realized that he really did have a family, a sister, even aunts and uncles if he wanted to get particular, at home. He was wanted, loved. There was nothing anywhere capable of competing with that.

When Travis had called with the news Chet had died, he'd accepted his dad would never have apologized. And it had been proven over and over by writing him out of any portion of inheritance of the ranch.

He hoped for the sake of those dependent on the ranch, Kyle was able to run it properly. But as of that afternoon, it was no longer his problem.

He brushed down Sandy and filled his hay feeder. "See you in the morning." He patted the muscled neck and closed the gate.

Nearing the side of the ranch house, he spotted the blue rental car parked out front. It gave zero clues.

He stomped his boots outside on the mat then walked through the door. "Marta!"

"Kitchen!"

He unbuttoned his jacket and walked down the hall. And froze to the floor when his gaze landed on the man standing there.

"Will?"

Will placed the steaming mug in his grip on the counter, uncertainty clouding his features. "I know I should have—" was as much as Parker let him say. He cleared the kitchen in long strides and grasped Will into his arms.

Will groaned, but even that was silenced as Parker claimed his lips, rocking them both with a need that wouldn't be denied. Will's hands dug underneath his jacket and fanned over Parker's spine, spiraling heat in all directions.

Parker raised a hand and with a flick of his wrist, he tossed his hat to the side, cupping Will within his palms to continue kissing him. Parker straddled his hips, caging him between his body and the counter. The hard press of body to body was driving him insane. He could happily explode from the rush of desire and longing that Will brought to the surface.

They were panting harshly when he lifted enough to meet Will's gaze. "Missed you. So much." Then he was kissing Will again. Parker didn't even care why he was there, how he'd managed it, or anything really, except that he was in his arms. They dueled for control, giving and taking. All Parker could do was feel. Will's hands roamed his frame, reaching for the ends of Parker's hair to grasp at it, to return to simply touching, kneading at skin with firm fingertips. Parker completely understood. He wanted to get his hands all over the man pressing into him like the other half of a sandwich cookie.

"Herd to base."

Parker released him reluctantly, panting. "Nosy bastards."

Will trembled. Parker didn't move an inch. He liked Will best right where he was.

"Herd to base."

Parker desperately wanted to ignore the call.

Will's arms curled loosely around Parker's waist. "Answer him before he blows a gasket with curiosity. I'm fine."

Parker reached for the talkie and pushed the button to speak. "Go ahead."

"Everything okay?"

"It's perfect." Parker never dropped Will's gaze. Not once. "See you when you come in."

"Parker?" Travis' voice crackled, ignored.

He placed it back in the cradle. He didn't know when Marta had vanished, but he was grateful for her timely need to be somewhere else. Soft hair separated between his stroking fingers. Parker smiled when he felt Will's fingers innocently glide downward to fill his rear pockets.

"I'm glad I found you. The ass at what I thought was your place was one of the rudest—"

Parker leaned and kissed him into silence. "Until about three this afternoon, I had a stake in the ranch, but my dad willed it to his last foreman. I'm sorry you had to deal with him."

"You mean... I thought something else entirely when you said he'd changed the will."

"Nope." He caressed the side of Will's neck, dancing fingers over a strong shoulder and down his body to finally hook the waist of his jeans. "Everything I want is in Jasper." Parker shivered as a rush of pleasure danced over his shoulders when those seeking fingers in his pockets flexed. "Well, almost everything."

The confused furrow on Will's brow was adorable.

"The most important thing is right here." He kissed Will softly, Will's lips puffy and red from the tangled kisses they'd shared. "Want you so much." He rested cheek to cheek, simply breathing in the scents that were Will. "I did the test on Monday." He couldn't remember if he'd mentioned it before he'd left on the bus or not.

"When will you know?"

"Hopefully next week."

Will groaned. "I know it's for the best, but I hate it."

Parker chuckled. "You and me both. So glad you're here."

"Good surprise?" Will asked, that breathless quality hitting his voice again when Parker started to nibble and nuzzle at his chin.

"The best surprise," Parker replied.

"Why *chulo papi*?" Will asked a few moments later.

"Because Travis is big *papi*. Apparently, I'm the cuter one."

"No arguments here," Will agreed. "I think you're amazing."

Parker straightened slowly. "You do?"

"After everything you've been through, to be where you are right now? I think you're one of the most levelheaded, incredible, kindhearted men I've ever known."

"And the age gap doesn't bother you anymore?"

Will tugged him until there wasn't an inch of breathing space between their bodies, ridges grinding, sending shocks of need into his blood.

"Sweetheart, I've met men twice your age who weren't half as mature. You do what's right. You treat others with respect, even the ones who haven't earned it. I…" Gray eyes met his, exposing everything, hiding nothing. "It's why I came. To be with you. Because it's where I belong, with you."

Parker thought he might have been about to admit something else, yet what Will *was* saying made his mouth dry, his body ache, and his heart trip into his ribs like a drunk cat on stairs.

Will cared enough to be there for him. To be there to get through this weekend.

It was more than Parker had ever thought he'd find. He was more than Parker had ever thought he could have. He never dreamed he'd be worthy of a man like Will.

Will may not be ready, or able yet, but Parker knew the truth. All those emotions and cravings had formed into one big ball of emotion.

He was in love with the man in his arms.

Chapter Twenty

Saturday started dull and overcast. Adding in the windy cold of the Texas gulf coast compounded the misery. There wasn't a long graveside service for Chet Vandersoot. Only a handful of men, Parker among them, deigned to consider his death significant enough to pay their respects.

Kyle, Dawson, and a few others from both ranches.

Parker, Will, Travis and Eddie were the rest. All total, less than a dozen men. Chet's funeral wasn't being given public media attention. The retired rodeo legend had met his end, and the day was receiving no acknowledgements from anywhere.

Parker was actually glad of that fact. The whole process took less than an hour.

"Any last words, Parker?" the preacher presiding over the funeral asked.

Parker glanced to Will, who squeezed his hand in answer. He hadn't realized until he woke in the same bed that morning how much he appreciated having him there to get him through today. "A few."

Will nodded once, pride softening his eyes.

Parker walked forward. He held his hat in his hands as he had since they'd first approached the site. Damp air and damper grass made it feel like he was in a bubble. One he was more than ready to leave behind. "I want to thank you for being here. I don't have a lot to say past that. I imagine a few of you may have a good memory or two, but I don't. Just thank you, for showing him the respect he never showed me."

He rejoined Will who quickly and unashamedly grasped his hand.

"You're twice the man he ever imagined himself to be."

"That's for damn sure," Travis muttered.

"I don't know how you can speak like that about the dead." Kyle glared.

"Easy. It's the same way I spoke when he was alive. He was no man to admire."

"He was a good man!"

Parker sighed. He knew he was just saying that because Chet had left literally everything to him, and he was idolizing a false image. If he had half the knowledge Parker did... "Would a good man beat his son? Would a good man disown his only child, kick him out of the only home he knew with nothing more than the clothes on his back?"

"You're gay," he retorted snidely.

Parker started to reply when Dawson stepped up. "And that don't make a bit o' difference. I *knew* what his daddy did, and he all but shot me to get rid of me when I took him to task over it. Chet was a mean, selfish bastard who thought more of himself than any other person on this planet. As I see it, Parker has done more for you than that old man ever did. He didn't take away your home when he coulda, he didn't kick you out on the street, when he coulda." He tipped his hat to Parker. "Think about it, you'll see the truth." He faced Travis. "See you back at the ranch."

"We'll be there soon."

Dawson and about half of the crowd split off to load pickup trucks and leave the cemetery.

Kyle left right after. It didn't surprise Parker that he was alone. He had a feeling before long he would be the *only* man left running the ranch.

"He'll never accept it," Eddie offered sadly.

"He's blind to the truth of who Chet really was." Parker turned and walked a few steps to stand at the coffin's side. He spoke quietly, solemnly. This was all he had left to say.

"Well, Dad. You got what you wanted. I'm out of your life. Whatever you hoped would happen to me, I don't know, but you failed. I have the family you never were. I have a sister who I'd bust skulls for. I have a boyfriend who I love more than that land and legendary image you were so proud of. I hope you got what you wanted. It was hard, but I know I am a better man than you'd ever hoped to be."

He scattered a single scoop of dirt onto the lid and dusted his hands off over it. Leaving his past there, along with all his pain, in the dirt.

* * * *

Will stayed apart, letting him say his piece. He knew this was very personal and probably long overdue. Travis and Eddie waited as well. When Parker joined him, Will clasped his hand. "Ready?"

His lips thinned for a heartbeat, then he relaxed. "Let's go."

"Parker says you've been learning how to ride, Will," Travis said a few minutes later from the front of the truck, driving them to the ranch. The sporadic swish of the wipers were the only interruption up to then.

"I'm getting there."

"Want to go play with the cows?"

Will swallowed, his skin prickling. "Like around the herd?" It sounded exciting and frightening all at once.

"Don't worry," Parker said at his shoulder. "Won't let anything happen to you." He cuddled up close, still holding Will's hand in a tight grasp. He hadn't let go at all.

Will turned on his neck, burying his nose under the length of hair at Parker's nape. He'd never been in this kind of situation where something was physically and out of necessity keeping him from getting closer. Definitely didn't like it. Desire and need for the cowboy beside him burned through his blood.

"If I get more time with you, I'd love to," he replied, his lips caressing Parker's flesh.

A quiet groan and a shiver was Parker's reaction. Lashes lowered over expressive eyes. A telling quiver struck Parker's lip. It was an image of an aroused Parker that would be locked away forever.

"Guys," Travis chided, laughing. "Uh. Not alone here."

Will blinked, and met Travis' humored gaze in the rearview mirror. "Only until you're not driving." He didn't want to risk them all because he wanted more of the man at his side.

"Fair enough."

He whispered into Parker's ear. "Can*not* wait for those results. I'm going to spend hours with you naked."

Parker whined low in his throat. Then he said, "What if... What if it says...I'm positive?"

Will heard the slight hitch in his question, the words tinged with a real fear.

"We'll deal with it." Will was staying hopeful. Parker was in great health even *after* the four years of hell he'd lived through.

"Will." He clasped his fingers tightly, his expressions changing on a dime, giving broad hints to the turmoil plaguing him.

"Shh," Will breathed below his ear. "Can't change anything today. I want to be with you."

Parker gazed at him with bottomless eyes. Bands of sunlight broke through the heavy cloud cover, washing Parker's features in its golden warmth. He didn't believe in divine intervention, or the will of God, but he did believe in intuition.

Will didn't know how he knew, but right then, he did. Parker was going to be fine.

He caressed his shaved chin with fingertips.

He also realized the very idea of not being with this man left him feeling hollow. The words were on the tip of his tongue. Three words he couldn't take back. Will had tried to keep his heart from falling for the strong man beside him.

He wasn't terribly upset that he'd failed.

The truck slowed and made a turn. Bumping from asphalt to driveway distracted him to look out the window.

They were arriving at the ranch.

"Look, baby," he whispered, motioning beyond Parker's shoulder.

Parker turned on the seat, then leaned close to Will who cradled him. A thick, very clear rainbow glowed in the distance as the clouds separated.

"Wonder if there's a pot of gold," Parker mused. Will knew there was. He'd found it.

* * * *

"Parker, you have mail," Ian called on Thursday the following week.

Will had been busy this week with Dr. Kirkpatrick, finalizing the legal transfer of the dental office. There hadn't been time for lessons, but the worst was Parker hadn't seen him at all since the previous weekend spent together in Texas.

He joined Ian in the kitchen. His heart was pounding. He knew what it would be. There was only one thing coming to the house that he knew of.

"You okay?" Ian studied him with patient kindness.

Parker had stopped dead in the middle of the kitchen. "Yeah. I'm fine." He stared blankly at the envelope in his hand, the return address finally registering. "I take that back," he whispered. "I'm terrified."

"Did you ever use a needle?"

"Never," he croaked. "But I wasn't an angel."

Ian held out an arm. "Come here."

Parker shook but succumbed to the offered kindness. Tremors rocked his frame where he pressed into Ian's strength.

"The longer you wait, the scarier it's going to be." Ian held him close, comforting him.

"I don't want to lose Will."

"Remember when you moved in here, and I said you need to let Caleb decide for himself?" Will nodded. "You need to give Will the same respect. He cares about you."

Parker drew a deep breath. "You're right." He swept a hand over his face and stepped clear. "It's not going to change anything it says by waiting longer, will it?"

"Afraid not," he agreed.

Parker ripped into the top of the envelope and withdrew the page. The words swam as he tried to focus. The terror he'd been fighting to keep at bay popped like a balloon as the medical results stopped blurring enough to make sense.

"Holy shit!" he cried as realization became crystal clear.

Ian reached for him and Parker all but leaped on him.

"Thankyouthankyouthankyou!"

"I take it it's good news?" Ian squeezed him tight.

"It is! Fuck! I have to tell Will!"

"Glad for you, Parker." Ian gave him another good, solid squeeze. He roughed Parker's hair when he let him go. "You're a good kid. I'm glad it didn't say otherwise."

Parker pushed Ian away playfully. "I'm twenty-one. Not a kid." Then he jumped on Ian again, dancing around the kitchen ruining the whole effort of mature independence. "You're the best!"

"Glad we could help you, Parker. We both are." He grasped Parker by the shoulders and steadied him a few seconds later when he teetered and wobbled on loose legs. "Your father may have been the man you came from, but you're one hell of a son. You've got a lot going for you."

Parker swallowed, his throat feeling tight with emotion. "I wouldn't be here at all if it weren't for you, Caleb, and Grint stopping that day. I'll never be able to repay all you've done, the whole family."

"Well, see, that's where you're wrong." Ian smiled, crossing his arms to lean against the kitchen counter. "You don't owe us for being family."

He glanced down, blinking hard. "So... I really belong? You want me to stay?"

"For as long as you want. Jasper could use a good man like you. And if I understand Will's barn idea right, you're both going to be doing a good thing for Jasper before too long."

"We have ideas. A lot will have to wait until spring."

"If you want to do continuing education, check with your Uncle Brice. I'm sure he can get you management courses and business stuff to look at."

"Uncle Brice." Parker smiled. "I like that. Will he mind?"

"That man lives to teach."

"I *did* kind of get that feeling from him," Parker joked.

Ian laughed. "Then you know everything you need to know about him." A car door slammed out front. "And there's the other half. I love these earlier days he's getting right now."

"Maybe they'll become permanent for him," Parker offered optimistically.

The front door opened. "Babe."

"Maybe. Hopefully." He sauntered out of the kitchen. When silence reigned for several minutes, Parker remained behind, giving them a few minutes of *them* time. It was the least he could do.

Chapter Twenty-One

Will was exhausted. Lawyers and contracts, legal notices and licenses. Transferred information, insurance and records from Florida. It was a lot of detailed work taking over for John. No matter how harrowing it became, it was what he needed, what he wanted. All he had to remember was that he was grateful for the opportunity to become a part of Jasper, which he was, and all the stress melted away, for a little while, anyway.

Rolling to a stop in front of the house, he almost groaned. This was the kind of day Parker had warned him about. Long hours, exhausted physically and mentally, but the animals in the barn needed him. He had stalls to check, feeders to fill.

And at some point, dinner.

He wanted to curl up in a ball right there on the front seat of his car.

Instead, he tiredly trudged from his car to the house, unlocking the door to be greeted by the warm accents that he adored. Rough hewn beams across the ceiling were stained to avoid rot. The color matched the wood flooring, darker by a shade or two since the floors had been subject to many more years of wear. That was on the to-do list for the spring. Now that the sale was happening, he could plan for things he wanted to touch up.

After changing out of his work scrubs, he donned a thick sweater over his shirt that he could remove if he got overheated while working in the barn. With a jacket over that to stay warm outside, he cleared the distance from his back door across the flat to the barn.

White clouds streamed around him with each breath. Temperatures were growing brisk at night. He hoped they could get the barn up to par to keep the animals safe in time.

Walking inside, he drew a breath. It was still pungent, but far less shocking than that day in August at the rodeo.

He paused inside the doorway, listening, amazed when he heard low spoken dialogue.

"Telling the horses bedtime stories now?" Will teased as he drew near.

"Will!" Parker dropped the brush in his hand. He huffed when he picked it up. "I wasn't expecting you yet."

"Why not?" He walked closer.

"Because it's only... Oh." Parker laughed when he looked around. "I lost track of time. I didn't realize it was that late."

"What do you have left?"

"Just need to make sure everyone has water." He finished brushing out Tank's mane. "I already brushed out Isis. I knew you'd been busy this week."

"Understatement," he muttered.

"I was also looking around. The heating won't be as big an issue as we thought."

"Oh?"

"Let me finish him, and I'll show you."

Will went around the stalls and checked on the animals, one by one, making sure the stalls were clean, feeders were filled with hay, and their water troughs were full. The detailed care was up to the owners, but the barn upkeep was on him, and now

Parker. And it looked like Parker had already gone through the whole barn like a tsunami, cleaning each stall and well.

"How long have you been here?"

"A couple of hours. Ian dropped me off."

"On top of being at the auto shop?" He was still going like he'd just bounced out of bed. Parker bit his lip to not grumble. These days would pass for him.

"Yeah, but I'm done there tomorrow. Saturday, I'll be here all day and every day after."

Will followed taut leg muscles and the way they flexed as Parker walked around Tank, finishing up his grooming. "Okay, boy. Bedtime." He herded Tank into his stall and gave him a sound pat on the neck. Digging a carrot chunk out of his pocket as a last thing, he put his riding buddy to bed.

Will noticed the affection he showed for the large gelding. He was glad they'd paired up so well. He knew Leslie was thankful for the help.

"Let me show you." Parker gathered the curry brush and hoof pick he'd been using. "Did the owner ever walk you through the barn?"

"Not really. Some, but since I wasn't using it when I occupied the rental, it wasn't a must-know detail."

Parker dropped his things into a large bucket. "Well, you're in luck." Will followed at his shoulder as he moved deeper into the tack room to a little alcove. "This is the fuse box for the barn." He opened a panel. "And this..." He flipped a switch. "Is the control to your heating. It's a low-degree infrared system."

"What does that mean?"

"It means it will glow with an infrared light that heats a surface, rather than using a heat blower.

Those can cause respiratory problems with airborne particles. It also keeps everything from getting super heated."

"Wow." He leaned closer to examine the control panel. "They're that sophisticated?"

"The better ones are. The barn may not be super new, but this is. After I found this, I noticed the tubes. I'll show you where they are, so you know."

"God, am I glad I hired you."

Parker grinned. "Glad to help."

"You are. Honestly, I was dreading facing this tonight. Not that I wouldn't but this has been a killer week with all the meetings."

Parker urged him out of the space. "Regretting it?" He closed the tack room door after them.

"No," he replied evenly, honestly. "I know there will be times like this. I'm just glad I have someone here who I trust, who knows what they're doing."

Parker put his hands in his pockets, his tread a little slower. "Just for the barn?"

Will paused at his side and saw the insecurity on Parker's face. "Not at all, cowboy." He leaned close and shared a tender kiss. "I guess I'm not being a very good boyfriend, am I? It was a nice surprise seeing you here, and realizing what you've done tonight... That you're taking care of Isis and Tank. That was the sweetest thing anyone has done all week."

"Bedding down your mare?" Parker stared at him askance.

"Just that." He slipped an arm around Parker's waist, bringing him tight into Will's side. "Let me get us both fed. You have a last day of work in the morning."

Parker tilted his head to touch Will's. "How much longer before you're done with all the red tape?" He nuzzled into Will's neck. "I miss our rides."

"Tomorrow should be it. I'm yours for the weekend."

Parker sighed in acceptance, warm breath ghosting over skin.

Will was never happier than when Parker copied him and wound a strong arm around him in return, walking together up to the house.

Once inside, Will unbundled himself, hanging his coat by the door. Parker's coat and hat joined it on the rack.

Was it foolish to like seeing them there?

He wasn't sure. He knew he cared. Without saying it yet, he *knew* how he felt. Parker had left everything to stay in Jasper. That had to mean something. And he was serious about the manager position if he was already a step ahead on the heating.

"I have pork chops already marinated. Can you wash the cauliflower?"

"Sure." Parker dug it out of the bottom of the fridge and after rolling up his sleeves to keep them dry, he ran it under the water, giving it a good scrub.

The silence was easy and since it wasn't as late as Will had feared it would have been, he didn't feel rushed either.

"I got the results today."

Five words. Will stopped what he was doing. His hands hovered over the platter, the meat instantly forgotten. Their relationship *did not* hinge on this. He'd already sworn that, to the both of them. He knew it didn't but he couldn't hide the small quiver of anxiety, just the same. A lot *could* change. And that was enough to make him nervous.

All the intuition on the planet couldn't stand up against reality.

Reality had arrived.

Will swallowed thickly, asking, "And?"

Parker finished at the sink, setting the soccer ball-sized vegetable on the dish rack to drip for a minute. He faced Will, and he *swore*, Parker prowled up to him.

Bright eyes refused to look away, keeping Will trapped.

"I hope you like having sex with your barn manager, because he definitely wants you."

Will moaned on an exhale. Relief rolled a shudder down his spine. Parker blanketed himself to Will's front and suddenly dinner really didn't seem all that important. He didn't open his eyes when Parker's lips slid over his, instead pushing upward almost insistently, wanting the heat of his kiss. He banded his arms around Parker's solid chest, clinging and kneading as kisses grew in strength. Will whined then. His heart pounded wildly with wanting.

He tugged, rocking against Parker and thrilling at the obvious hardness rolling against him.

Parker moaned, a low rumbled sound. The vibration shot goose bumps over Will's flesh.

Will was the first to break for air. "You're clean?" He wanted to hear the words.

"Clean bill of health," Parker replied, keeping him body to body close.

Will held him tight. "No more risks."

Parker seemed to understand the seriousness of Will's point, returning the embrace in solemn quiet.

"I know it means a lot for you, too," Parker said. "I don't want to risk either of us."

"I swear you're older than twenty-one," he said, caressing Parker beneath his hands. How could he care *that much* about Will's stake in it? Parker had to be the most unselfish, conscientious man Will had ever met.

"No risks goes for you too, you know. I know there's always a chance, because patients don't always share the information, or someone may not even know. Promise me you'll take every health precaution out there." He stroked with kind hands. "I want you to stay healthy, too."

"Will this work?"

"Working for you? Wanting you every second of every day?" Parker raised a cool hand and stroked Will's neck. "I really don't know. But I want the job. I trust you to pay me for the work I do. I think having the hot dentist for my boyfriend is a perk of the job."

Will snickered. "I guess that means..."

Parker leaned close, his lips resting above Will's. "I'm all yours."

"What now?" Will asked after another round of kisses that melted his thoughts. He still wanted, but he was beginning to suspect Parker had much better control than he did.

"Dinner. Then I guess you better take me home."

"Oh." He almost sobbed now that it was possible and he still had to wait. That really wasn't what he'd hoped to hear. Why did Parker have to be so mature about *everything*?

Parker smiled, as though he knew exactly what was plaguing Will. Maybe he did, considering.

"Just because I can, and it's safe, doesn't mean we need to right now. I'd love to, but it's late, and people will worry if I'm not home before too long. Plus you have a long day tomorrow."

"This weekend?"

Parker nipped lightly at Will's chin. "Talk to the barn manager when you see him. I'm sure he'll be willing to sneak away for a while."

"You're mean."

"No. I'm being sincere."

"Sincere?"

"I want this to work. All of it. The job. You. Me." He shared another lingering kiss. "I like all of this. Being here, being with you."

"And you don't want to rush anything?"

Parker kissed him again. "No."

"You're staying, right? In Jasper?"

"I'm staying. I'm home."

Will knew he couldn't keep pushing, no matter how much he ached or how tight his jeans were at that moment. Parker had solidified his words by his continued actions. He'd never said something and not followed through. If Parker said it, then he meant it.

"Okay. Then let's cook dinner and eat so I can get you home. I really don't want to be on either Caleb's or Ian's bad side."

Parker merely kissed him again before retreating to help finish prepping dinner.

Chapter Twenty-Two

Parker brushed Tank's coat on Saturday morning. The horses had their grain early that morning so they were ready. The barn was clean. The boarders were out. It was a beautiful December day to ride. Crisp, with a golden sun in the sky.

All he was missing was—

"Whose car is that?"

Parker hunted over Tank's withers, smiling now that the missing person had appeared. He knew Will meant the car he'd parked near the barn doors. He was pretty sure Ian had led him into the whole car conversation yesterday at the auto shop. He'd be needing transportation for his job and how he'd manage things now that he wouldn't be working on Ian's schedule. He didn't mind, not really. He'd learned quite a while ago that both Ian and Caleb could be devious, in a good-nurturing kind of way. "It'll be mine soon. I'm buying it from Caleb."

Will met him at Tank's shoulder and greeted him with a kiss. "Those two are amazing."

Parker grinned. "I know. He hasn't needed it much so they offered it to me."

"A decent price?"

"I think so. Ian's kept it running, so I know it's been well cared for."

Will stroked Tank's neck, plying fingers through the horse's mane. "You would rather buy it yourself than be handed a gift, wouldn't you?"

Parker slowed, his hand pausing midair with the curry brush. "I think it depends. Why?"

Will smiled shyly at him. "Something I've been debating. I think I'll let it stew for a while yet."

Parker tugged the man closer, grabbing a full throttle kiss. "You're just as amazing," he said when he let him go.

Will cleared his throat, heat flushing his cheeks with a redness that Parker had begun to recognize and adore.

"Let me get Isis' tack out and I'll start on her."

Parker watched his man as he cleaned up Isis and got her ready to ride. Dark hair glistened with morning sunlight coming through the barn doors. Will had grown comfortable and confident in the months he'd been learning how to ride. Isis had been a good match for him after all. Not too spunky, mild of nature with a huge heart.

Kind of like the man.

He rested the brush he was using on a shelf and slipped under Tank's head to wrap his arms around Will's waist.

His movements stuttered then stopped. "Hi there, cowboy."

Parker nuzzled into Will's shoulder. He loved the way Will smelled. It had to be his aftershave or something, but it wasn't like anything he could describe. A small shiver rolled down Will's frame when he found flesh with lips. Will tipped, encouraging more. Parker wasn't going to deny him.

Parker's breathing sped up when Will pressed backward, rubbing in slow circles against Parker's front.

"I vote we postpone the ride for a few hours." Now that Parker was holding him, he really didn't want to let go. Ever.

"I don't know," Will replied breathily. "I might need more than a few hours to enjoy this."

Parker laughed at his playfulness. "Let's turn them out for now. We can go tonight..." He nibbled again. "Tomorrow." *Any time.* Another one of those lovely perks.

"I guess one ride is as good...as another." Will panted, leaning against Parker.

"Funny man, Doc." He nibbled for a few seconds more then let him free. He led Tank to the pasture and unclipped the rope from the halter, giving him a sound swat on the rump. Isis quickly followed once she realized there was *outside* today.

"We'll clean up later." Parker took both leads and hung them from a hook by one of the stalls, then he grabbed one of Will's hands.

He hoped he wasn't coming on too strong, but he couldn't help himself. It was like everything had aligned. He was moving forward again with his life, and this time with Will. To him, that was just about perfect.

Once inside, they hung up coats, sharing teasing kisses between them. Once boots were tugged off, Parker stalked Will in socked feet. He followed a beckoning Will from the rear door down the hallway. Will backed into a bedroom.

All that mattered right that minute was the bed coming into view.

Blood rushed through his veins watching Will tug his heavy sweater over his head. Parker didn't see a man who was almost ten years older than himself.

He saw a man who was amazing to look at. A man who was beautiful inside and out.

Parker finished unbuttoning his shirt, pulling the tails out of his jeans waist, and closed the distance between them. With firm hands, Parker tugged Will's undershirt out of his jeans, making it pretty obvious what he wanted. Will complied, tossing the light undershirt away. Parker ran his hand from shoulder to waist, enjoying the feel of fluttering skin beneath his palm. He couldn't resist licking lightly at one of the needy tips. Will trembled on his feet, clutching with his fists. Not exactly satisfied but needing to see more of him, the button and zipper on Will's jeans were next.

Parker felt the brush of knuckles against his stomach and glanced down, catching Will repaying the favor.

He groaned when the release of fabric provided room.

"Better?"

"So much," Parker said, with a small gasp.

Will smiled sweetly. "Been wanting this for so long," he said, closing the gap between them to lick and nibble at Parker's chin. Parker found his lips. Then he was guiding Will backward.

When he hit the bed, Parker shucked Will's jeans to his ankles, never letting go of his kisses. Once Will was on the bed, Parker finished yanking off all their clothing.

Will raised a hand and touched, creating a wall of shivers over Parker's frame.

"Nice." Will stroked Parker's length, coaxing a low moan through his body. When Parker thought he would've let go, he tugged instead, bringing him onto the bed with a playful splat. "Even better," he said, laughing warmly, wrapping him into caring arms.

Playful kisses grew into passionate forays. Will roamed his fingers into Parker's hair. He repaid the sensual teases by stroking over his abdomen and upper thighs. Skin to skin that burned. When Will didn't push for more, didn't try to take the lead, Parker shifted. He raised to speak, panting with the words getting lodged somewhere in his throat. Will understood. He pointed to the nightstand by the bed.

Digging around in the drawer, he quickly found what he wanted. He pressed against Will's length on the bed. His heart tripped now that he was faced with *the moment*. "I've only driven once," he said.

"Are you comfortable doing it?" Will touched his face, caressing him with light fingertips.

"I think so."

"I don't have a problem...if you'd rather. This time." That sweet smile, powered by the lone dimple, had Parker feeling lightheaded.

Parker neared and kissed him patiently, expressing what he couldn't find the words to say. With that decided, he couldn't stop touching skin. Couldn't stop kissing him as his need and desire flared brighter than ever before.

The rush was incredible, the heat addictive as he tenderly prepared the man on the bed. Short pants and moaned gasps directed him, and when he found that one spot, Will's entire body vibrated.

"Love that," he crooned.

"Parker." Will was grasping at the bed, insistently rolling his body toward him.

Parker covered and slicked his length. He caressed the roundness in front of him as Will opened up, lifting his legs behind his knees. He took his time, letting Will catch his breath as he inched closer. Glistening skin had darkened to a deep, aroused pink, flexing in anticipation.

There was the slightest pause that he couldn't hide, his anxious gaze flipping back and forth between where they touched and Will's features.

A flex and he swore his heart stopped. His head hung loose on his neck for a span of seconds, overwhelmed by the heat, the pressure as he sank inward for the first time. He surged slowly forward when he could think, watching Will. All he saw was need, patient and wanting.

Slow strokes brought them closer and closer until Parker was pressed right up to Will's body.

"Still okay?" He did have enough mental ability to ask that at least.

"Watching the most gorgeous man in my life," he rasped. Hard breaths rocked his chest. Then he rolled his hips, telling Parker he was ready for more.

As his conscious thinking capacity shrank, his body took over, slowly loving the man watching him through lowered eyelashes. Slow strokes became waves of passion, his heart, mind, and body completely Will's.

Will must have sensed he was going to fall over the cliff soon. He began to tug on his shaft, rolling his cockhead against his palm to stroke the full length with Parker's pace.

Gray eyes glittered with desire, burning through Parker's soul. There was a grunt paired with a tremor that rocked them both. Will dug his head into his pillow, arching as his hips flexed. The most amazing thing Parker had ever witnessed happened. The full-bodied orgasm of the man he loved.

The tightness surrounding him claimed him, sucked him in and he groaned, thick and long. Energy raced down his spine, tickling nerves right behind his nuts. It drove him crazy feeling the pressure. Bright flares that filled his vision until his body exploded. The flutter of muscle, the clench of heat, and the sound of Will's echoed heaves for air were the perfect storm.

Boneless, he eased away from Will and sank to the bed at his shoulder. The condom started to slip and he caught it.

Will's chuckle was rough. "There's a can...somewhere." He waved a limp hand to the side. "It was there this morning."

Laughing with him, Parker sat up on the edge and spotted it. Disposing of the condom, he cleaned up as much as he could with tissues from the nightstand. He was pretty sure Will didn't keep them there for movie nights. He smirked at his man, but kept his guesses to himself. "Do you need to clean up?"

"Yeah," Will replied, a little less breathless. "Want to go share a quick shower?"

Parker nodded. "I'd love to."

Will smiled for him, unleashing that dimple. "Good," he whispered. Threading fingers into Parker's hair, he brought Parker to his lips. It took several lingering minutes for either to gather enough energy to actually do something about that shower, though.

Chapter Twenty-Three

Late Christmas morning, Parker sauntered from the barn to the house, avoiding the larger snow and ice clumps that were now winter dormant grass. In the few weeks he'd been in charge of the barn, this had become a routine. Days Will was at home, after Parker was done with the upkeep and business outside, he met with Will for coffee and kisses inside. He wasn't huge on the coffee, but try to keep him from getting his morning kisses.

Will was in the process of equipping one of the smaller bedrooms into an office for Parker, a roomier, convenient means to help him stay on top of the work involved and all the numbers, income, and supplies.

It meant he'd be coming and going frequently, a situation Will said he was fine with. The two of them together were beginning to make quite the team when it came to the horses and plans for the future.

Their future. There had been some discussion, but not a lot. Not yet. Parker was glad Will had taken it to heart when he said he wanted to take his time. He could see a lot happening between them, in the years to come. He wanted to see it all become a reality. One thing he'd learned even at his young age, was you couldn't rush life. This was good. No, this was great between them and he wanted to keep going. Moving forward.

The boarding part of his responsibilities was staying steady. Because of that, it looked like in the spring they'd be able to implement a core riding class that Parker could teach. He wasn't going to sit idle for six or more hours a day. He came in the mornings to handle the stalls and the feedings, and then again in the evening for any care. The middle of the day was wide open. This would be his contribution to making the stable a success. A business that he personally could manage and oversee.

They would be bringing in four or five ponies and smaller horses to use for the classes. He was excited about the whole idea. A program that they'd fine tune over the winter.

He hadn't told her yet, but Summer was going to be one of his first guinea pigs. He knew she'd be over the moon for the chance. The girl had been talking horses—and to her mothers' dismay, bulls—since the rodeo.

He stomped his boots outside on the mat and hung his coat and hat on the rear hooks by the door. Walking down the hall, he found Will's door was closed. He tapped with a knuckle.

"Be right there!"

"Are you decent?"

"Uh… Can you wait in the kitchen? I'll be right there. I promise!"

Parker's brow bunched up. That was a first. He hadn't sounded mad or anything, but it still confused him. Usually that was where the first kisses started. "Okay."

He tried to not scuff his feet walking to the kitchen in disappointment. He guessed he'd have to wait Will out.

The coffeepot was full, so he *had* been up for a little while already. When he turned the other way, he noticed a white box on the table. It was tied closed simply with a thin, red ribbon. Walking closer, he spotted the little tag hanging off the end with his name on it.

The sound of boots on hardwood had him swiveling. "Wow," he gasped when his gaze fell on the stud coming closer.

Will stood there utterly decked out. A crisp western shirt with pearl snaps. Dark blue jeans, freshly polished boots and a black calfskin belt with a small oval buckle to finish it off. The best part was the cowboy hat. "You look amazing."

Will's lips tightened and twitched as he fought a smile. Pleasure warmed his cheeks. "You think so?"

Parker walked forward. "Hot. Would never believe five months ago you were a beaching city guy." He crossed the space between them and tugged Will tight into his chest. "Gorgeous," he added before devouring Will's kiss.

Neither was breathing steadily when they released. "I have to see. Let me see if those jeans do your ass justice."

Will snickered but stepped back and turned around, running his palm down a cheek teasingly.

"Yeaaaah. Those are going to cause bar fights." Parker hooked a belt loop and yanked him backward right into his arms. "Good thing you have me." He bit at an earlobe until Will whined.

"Par-*ker*."

"Hm?"

"So I pass inspection?"

Parker chuckled, burying his nose in Will's shoulder to hide it. "And then some. What's the special occasion?"

"Because we're going riding."

Parker studied Will's clothing, already envisioning all the things that could ruin them. He popped open his mouth, Will turning in his arms to catch him, grinning at him while humor made his gray eyes sparkle. Just like Ian could with Caleb, he bet Will could read his mind.

"Just this once. These are going out clothes. But I like it when you think I'm hot."

"You always are."

"And now I have the right cheese to catch my mouse."

Parker groaned, his chest rocking with suppressed laughter.

"The only thing is, we need horses."

Parker hummed, playing along. "Okay, cowboy. Where do we get horses?"

Will stretched without losing Parker's grip and palmed the white box. "I don't believe in Christmas but I believe in sharing. I hope you like it."

Unsure, Parker let his hands fall from around Will to take the box. Untying the red ribbon bow, it slipped off. The length fell in a stream to the table.

Opening the box, he pulled out a gold plaque. Tank was written in bold letters, with smaller letters underneath. The smaller print read: Owner: Parker Vandersoot.

"Will... How? Why?"

"Well, I had to be a tiny bit devious. Remember when I said Leslie needed help with him?" Parker nodded, gazing with wonder at the shiny metal, running his fingers over the scored letters. "She was actually going to cancel her contracts because she couldn't afford upkeep for two horses. We worked out a deal. I bought Tank so she could afford Buster. She likes having him here. Knows they're both well cared for and safe. Even if you hadn't liked him, I would have kept him."

"So..." Parker's one eyebrow arched.

"Soooo." Will took his hat off and rested it upside down on the table. "I hope you'll go riding with me today. On your horse."

"He's really mine?"

"I have the bill of sale ready to sign him over to you whenever you can spare ten seconds."

"You've been working on this for months, haven't you?"

"A couple. I wasn't sure after your dad's funeral how you'd take this kind of well-meaning interference. I hope you not screaming and cussing me out is a good sign." Will gazed at him with questioning, expressive eyes.

"Will, baby. I'd never do that to you." He corralled the hesitant man into his body with an arm around his shoulders. He let out a slow breath and placed the new plaque by Will's brand new hat. "I can't thank you enough for everything. You make me the happiest I've been in so long." He nibbled at Will's lips, feeling the slight dryness from being out in the cold so much. The air was dryer at the dental office too because of the cold. Honestly, he didn't care. All that mattered right that second was Will, and what he was saying. "Yes, I want to ride with you. Every day. For the rest of our lives."

Will's breathing staggered. "I love you, Parker. I know you're not ready to move in. I understand that, but I'm telling you, now, today, I love you, and someday soon, I want to be able to wake up with you in that bed. I want to hear you grumbling about having to go feed in a five AM rainstorm. I want to share the good moments and the bad. I want to spend every waking and sleeping minute I can have with you."

Parker's throat had tightened up. Once Will got going, he didn't have a single word he could say to slow him down. So much for the quiet man he'd always thought him to be.

"I'm not going anywhere, especially now." He tipped Will up by the chin to meet the most endearing gray eyes. "Because I love you, too. I knew it in Texas, but I was so scared." He bit down on his lower lip, taking a moment. He'd never been especially good at speaking from the heart. Hopefully this time, he got it right. "It hasn't been easy, and I've had a world of doubts, but finding myself in Jasper has been the best thing. The best thing I've found *here*...is you."

They shared a few tender kisses, Will's fingers winding into his hair. Parker had discovered that was one of his most favorite things to do, and until he turned old and gray, he'd wear it long enough to keep his man happy.

"How about a hot breakfast before we tackle that December cold?"

"I like that idea. We'll take a nice ride, then come home and warm up in a hot shower."

Will nuzzled into his chin. "And if other things happen along the way..."

"Oh, I'm pretty sure *other things* are going to happen frequently."

"Yay me," Will cheered quietly. He ghosted a few more lingering kisses before stepping away. "Food, or we won't even make it out of the house."

Parker smirked, knowing better than to argue. When Will turned away, for good measure and because Parker couldn't resist, he ran a hand down Will's backside, goosing him gently.

Laughter from the both of them, deep and carefree, filled the kitchen. It would be the first of many, many, wonderful shared mornings if Parker had his way.

Now... If he could figure out how to bring kids into the conversation...

About the Author

Diana DeRicci is the sexy, flirty pen name of Diana Castilleja. A romance author at heart, DeRicci's writing takes you into a saucier spectrum of sensuality and sexual adventure, where a happily-ever-after is still the key to any story. Diana lives in Central Texas with her husband, one son, and a feisty little Chihuahua named Rascal. You can catch the latest news on all of Diana DeRicci's writing and books on her website. Feel free to drop Diana an email. She'd love to hear from you.

Visit her on the web at:
www.DianaDeRicci.com

PURPLE SWORD PUBLICATIONS
www.purplesword.com